THERE WILL BE
THORNS

By

Fox Jones

First Edition

ISBN: 979-8-9857316-2-0

Published by: Delphine Legacy Media

Cover design by: Web Presence Designs
Edited by: Molly Rupp

Printed in USA

For information, contact:
info@delphinelegacymedia.com

I call upon the ancestors
From near and far
Both remembered and forgotten
To hear us in our hour of need.

Look down upon us
If we are found worthy in your eyes
Send your mercies and healing
To my brothers and sisters in arms.

Great Ancestors from beyond the veil
Send their spirit back from the void
Their time came too soon
Their work has not finished.

Flow through me to heal their wounds
Help me guide them back from the shadows
And return their light to the land of the living.

We lay these gifts
At your feet in gratitude
May you find us worthy and answer our prayer.

Table of Contents

Dedication

For my three sons — my lions, my proof that strength doesn't mean the absence of softness. You are the roots beneath every thorn.

Acknowledgments

To my family — thank you for grounding me through every late night, long sigh, and rewrite that demanded more heart than sleep. You are my anchor and my calm.

To my readers and supporters — your words, your messages, your loyalty breathe life into DS Enterprises and the shadows it casts. Every theory, every gasp, every quiet moment you spend in this world means more than I can say.

To my project manager and the incredible team who walked this path with me — thank you for shaping chaos into clarity, for your patience, precision, and faith that this story could bloom through every thorn.

And to everyone who has rebuilt themselves after loss — may you find beauty in your scars, strength in your silence, and power in your return.

Author's Note

This story was never about perfection—it was about survival. Every operative, every choice, every silence carries the weight of what it costs to endure. *There Will Be Thorns* grew from the same soil as *When the Tiger Lily Blooms,* but the bloom is different now—sharper, more deliberate, more aware of what must be lost to be found again.

To those who walk the line between duty and desire, between loyalty and love, I see you. And to those still learning how to grow through the wreckage—keep going. There is beauty here, even among the thorns.

PART I

The Game Behind the Gilded Trap

Every snare begins with a shimmer. Every move, a promise disguised as choice.

CHAPTER 1

The Smoke Lingers

The flight from Amsterdam back to the Complex was as slow as a turtle making its way back to sea. The tragic extermination of Raven replayed in my mind, an endless loop. I mean, finding out your supposed best friend killed your real best friend and then made it look like a suicide while trying to convince you to murder your mentor is crazy business. On top of that, you find out the supposed best friend was a double agent who tried to kill you once you uncovered the plot? Yeah, she had to go. Her demise and the reasoning gave me some comfort as I shifted in my seat.

As I tried to get comfortable, Pearl reached out and squeezed my shoulder. "Hey. Just breathe. Remember your breathing exercises and relax." I put in my earbuds and took deep breaths. I took out my notebook and scribbled some thoughts.

Thoughts of you flood my mind.
The memories we created will last forever.
No one knew me like you did.
No lover or sibling could touch you.
Or your status in my heart.

This is why it hurts.
Like popping a cyst and watching the pus ooze…

The plane tossed in the air, causing me to stop writing. I gulped twice to regain focus. I didn't know if I wanted to cry because of the pain I experienced by killing my best friend or because I was relieved the Pack no longer existed. I glanced over at Pearl, who had her own headphones on and was watching an episode of Golden Girls. She paused the episode to check her messages. She groaned and resumed her episode. While I continued to write, I wondered why Pearl wasn't my handler the entire time. I daydreamed about how different the assignments would have been. How much I would've learned. I put away my notebook, turned on some tunes, and closed my eyes. After the day I had, I hoped I'd find some type of Zen.

The rubber of the tires smacking the runway jarred me out of my sleep. I stretched my legs and glanced over at Pearl, who was stowing her laptop. The plane came to an abrupt halt, and the crew opened the doors. Pearl stood up and walked towards the exit. I took off my seat belt and darted after her. We breezed through customs and walked straight to the parking garage. She pulled a key fob out of her pocket and signaled our car.

The car purred as we both slid into the front seats. Pearl put on her sunglasses, took the wheel, and sped away. Damn, I didn't even have enough time to buckle my seat belt as she careened through the streets and took little side roads as if we were qualifying for the Daytona 500.

"Why are we in such a hurry?" I held on to the side door handle, praying for our safety.

"Considering what's happened, we're scheduled to debrief the boss and the department in 30 minutes. It would behoove us to not be late." Pearl kept her eyes on the road as she explained. "Usually, you and I meet with the analyst team with the who, what, where, and how of the assignments and the team briefs the Operations boss. But because this case includes a double agent, we'll be briefing the analyst team, the big boss, the deputy boss, and the CEO."

"Wow! I knew there was some type of hot wash after each of our assignments, but I wasn't expecting to debrief this soon!" The grip on the side door handled loosened, but I still prayed to the ancestors for our safe arrival.

"That's right! This is your first debrief. All I can say is exaggerate nothing."

As Pearl snaked her way through the streets, my mind couldn't shake the fact I just killed my best friend. I thought I was a horrible friend to Emerald because she couldn't tell me about her trauma, but I now knew I was even more horrible because I couldn't see through Raven.

"You did nothing wrong." Pearl slowed down as she reached over and patted my hand. I smiled and let out a small sigh. She always knew how to help calm my thoughts.

Security waved us through as we pulled up to the Complex in record time. Pearl pulled up to a building in the rear and parked. We went inside and the security guard scanned our badges.

"Elevator 4, Level 6." He nodded towards the elevators after confirming our identity. We thanked him as we hopped on the elevator.

As the door closed, I felt a tide of nervousness roll over me. This was my first debrief. I didn't know what to expect. Breathe in. Close eyes. Hold one, two, three, four, five. Breathe out. Open eyes. On cue, I heard Pearl's voice cut through the anxiety.

"I must warn you, what you're about to hear is going to be hard. Trust me when I say we had your back the entire time."

I wanted to ask more questions, but the elevator came to an abrupt stop. The doors opened, and I saw Aster waiting for us with a couple of folders.

"Welcome back, Onyx. Pearl. If you would follow me, please." She handed each of us a folder and escorted us to the debriefing room.

CHAPTER 2

Silent Invitation

Aster punched in the code for the room to one of the more secure areas. Each of us had to use our badge to enter. Once the security measures were performed, the door opened and I scanned the surroundings. The room was a bland cloudy color with no windows. In the mi

ddle of the room, a round conference table was surrounded by standard chairs. The computer equipment included both a front and back screen so everyone could see the computer slides. Glacier sat at the head of the table with Ruby on her right and a person I didn't recognize on her left. My heart skipped a beat as I slid into my assigned seat. Pearl eased into a chair beside me.

Glacier powerwalked to me and gave me a hug. I returned it, all my feelings washing over me. For the first time that day, I felt safe. After the hug, Glacier returned to her seat. She grinned as she looked over the notes in her folder. It dawned on me she was wearing sunglasses inside the building. She took a deep breath and addressed us. "Onyx, Pearl. Glad you arrived safe and sound. Before we hot wash the incident, I want to introduce both of you to our new Director of Operations, Obsidian."

Obsidian raised her hand and nodded while Glacier continued. "She comes to us from the Navy as a Master Chief. Recently retired and her area of expertise is operations. Multiple deployments and assignments under her belt so she's well equipped to handle this department. When you get a chance, make sure you welcome her aboard."

We all murmured our greetings while Obsidian nodded. Glacier continued. "Sid, these are the two agents, Onyx and Pearl. Pearl was Onyx's trainer before being released to the field. Alex, aka Raven, called out sick, so Pearl accompanied Onyx at the European retreat house."

Sid nodded and spoke up. "Hello all. Glad to be a member of the team. And please, call me Sid." She took a sip of water and opened her notebook. "Now, Onyx. Tell us what happened."

My spirit shuddered. It was strange. I just met this woman and I got the same vibe I get from Glacier: tough, no nonsense, but there's some warmth. I cleared my throat.

"I left the retreat house per the instructions given to me by Raven. I was told it was time for another assignment, so I left the house and got on the train to catch the flight. I didn't think much of it because my assignments usually come later. While on the train, I received my package. It only had a picture of Glacier. There was no information. Just a picture. I found it odd and called Raven. Raven just told me to do what needed to be done and hung up. I knew something was wrong, so I texted Pearl. Pearl instructed me to go to the airport as planned and she would meet me there. She did warn me not to tell Raven." A lump formed in my throat, causing me to pause.

Sid gestured to the water pitcher. "Take your time. You can continue when you're ready."

I nodded as I filled my glass and gulped down the water. I exhaled. "When I met up with Pearl, we went to a secluded area in the airport. She confirmed my suspicions about my best friend and filled me in on everything that was happening. We came up with a game plan and I was one hundred percent on board. I went to the restroom to prepare, where I was ambushed by Raven."

The lump returned to my throat as I could feel the anger rise in my body like lava from a volcano. Then, as if in a trance, I regurgitated every single action from Raven's confession to both Emerald's murder and making it look like a suicide to using me to get rid of the Pack and ultimately Glacier. I ended my part with a detailed account of Raven's execution.

Sid scribbled my responses as the analyst typed. "At any time, did Alex's absence ever bother you?"

I took another sip. "I was new to everything and she was my best friend. She recruited me. She was there during Emerald's death. I didn't have a reason not to trust her."

Sid hummed to herself and stopped. "How do you feel now?"

"I'm at peace with how it went down. She deserved what she got. She murdered a sister and gave our enemy info about the organization and our members. I wished I had recognized it earlier. I may have been able to prevent later crimes."

Glacier stared at me from behind dark lenses. "Full disclosure—we had suspicions for a while. There were too many times you were left alone without explanation. Handlers never leave the operative. Because of this, we started to check her communications. The betrayal was confirmed when you went after Venom, which is why Wolverine was prepared when you were about to exterminate Raccoon. We weren't sure where you stood with Alex, so we gambled on you with the hope she would slip up and you would find out."

"I understand. I think that's the reason she felt comfortable enough to put a hit on you. I never asked questions and she assumed my loyalty was always to her. She didn't bank on Pearl, Citrine, and Wilhelm."

"She didn't bank on your intelligence and critical thinking skills. How did Citrine and Wilhelm find out?"

"They kept calling her Alex. They reminded me handlers never leave their operatives and no one in the organization is called by an animal name. Then I remembered animal names are reserved for targets. I'd hoped they were wrong."

Glacier stretched out in her seat. "I got all I need for this. Did anyone else have any questions?"

Ruby sat back in her chair and placed her hands on top of her head. "Take me through what happened with Venom."

Without missing a beat, I answered. "I was unhinged. I hated her to the point I used her children to torture her. I know as an agent, I must always stay in control. But when I ended her life, a weight came off my shoulders."

Ruby shrugged her shoulders as Glacier glanced over. "I read the report. I just wanted the audio version."

Glacier chuckled. "Last call? Pearl, do you have anything to add?" Pearl shook her head as Glacier continued. "First, Onyx, thank you for the debrief. I know you went through a rough time and retelling the events was taxing. But I want you to know you did nothing wrong. Alex betrayed your trust and was about to end your life when you saw through her. You did what you had to do for survival. Just know we are behind you, and you did nothing wrong."

I mouthed my thanks as Pearl squeezed my shoulder. "To be frank, that was the only thing on my mind. I knew I wasn't wrong killing Raven. I didn't want to be thrown out of the organization I consider family, where I found my purpose and myself."

Glacier cleared her throat. "I'm glad you consider us family. If there is nothing else, I'll leave you with Sid. Aster, I need the minutes of this debrief no later than tomorrow morning. Is that enough time?" Aster nodded her head as she wrote on her tablet. "Good. Sid?" Glacier and Ruby stood up and strolled out of the room, with Aster following close behind.

Sid took a seat across from Pearl and me. "Listen. I wanted to tell you both I'm very proud of you. And as much as I want y'all to work tomorrow and continue the work, you need to decompress. You both got thirty days to do just that. After thirty days when you get back, you need to make an appointment with Dr. Buho. If you choose to do it before you come back, that's fine. Once you have done this, you will report to me. Is there anything else you need from me?"

Pearl looked at me and I shook my head. I just wanted to get out of there and go to sleep. I then realized I didn't have a place to sleep.

As I was about to open my mouth, Sid put up her hand. "Go to the main building and see Ms. Magnolia. She'll give you your apartment keys. See you in thirty days." Sid got up and walked out of the room.

Pearl turned to me. "Talk to me."

I heaved a huge sigh. "It's crazy. I suspected but I never thought she would turn on me. I feel betrayed yet relieved. I knew Emerald didn't kill herself. And this ending provided redemption and closure."

The tears rolled down my face. Pearl let me have this moment without interruption. Her presence alone made me feel safe enough to let them fall.

After what seemed like hours, Pearl patted my shoulder. "Hey. It's time to pick up your apartment and car keys. I'll walk with you to the building."

I scrunched up my face. "Car keys? I thought I was just getting apartment keys."

Pearl shook her head. "Our new boss forgot to mention the car. Agents live in the community. You have to blend."

It sounded too good to be true. I felt compelled to question this. "So...not on the compound?"

Pearl roared with laughter. "You're full-fledged now. Agents live in the community. When they give you the keys, you will be met by one of the housing specialists to go over the apartment and the security system."

I nodded my thanks as we walked towards the main building. So much I'd learned but so much I still had to learn.

I don't remember how I got to the main building, but Ms. Magnolia didn't give me any keys for an apartment or for a car. Instead, she had me fill out a packet, which included questions about my favorite color, style, even scent. I hurried to fill it out and returned the packet. Ms. Magnolia fed the packet through a machine, which spit out a piece of paper. She reached over and handed me some keys.

"Here are your car keys. You need to sign here and here for ownership." She pushed a paper towards me with a pen and pointed out the places I needed to sign for the car. As I signed, she continued. "Your car is parked in the lower parking lot. Directions to the real estate agent are on the seat. Here's my number. Call me if you need anything. See you in a month." Ms. Magnolia handed me her card and grinned.

We found the car, a black Jeep Wrangler with black rims. I fell in love instantly. I hopped into the driver's seat and it roared to life. I appreciated the sound. Seeing the piece of paper on the passenger seat, I punched the address into the GPS and headed towards the real estate office. Pearl followed closely behind.

I tried not to think about what happened. I wanted to go on with my life. I knew Emerald would want that. I sighed as I pulled up to the real estate office. Pearl and I marched into the agency, and I met my leasing agent. I thought we were going to talk about my new digs. Instead she told me to follow her. After seven minutes of driving, we pulled up to a gated community. My leasing agent punched a code and drove through the gate before parking in front of a townhome. She jumped out of the car and beckoned me and Pearl to follow her. I rolled my eyes and met her inside.

After signing the paperwork, I was handed the keys to my condo.

"Good luck!" chirped the real estate agent. "Let me know if you need anything." Her bracelets jingled as she waved. Pearl glanced around, admiring the surroundings.

"I think you did very well here. I'm sure you'll like it." She walked over to the sliding glass door and stepped out onto the balcony.

I rubbed my temples. "I don't know. It's pretty big for just me." I followed her outside, feeling the space close in around me. It was cozy—but overwhelming.

"Whelp, lucky for you, you've got thirty days to take it all in. Rest up. Call if you need anything." She gave a short wave, then left.

And just like that, I was alone for the first time since I left the retreat house.

I sank to the floor. My vision blurred. My stomach twisted hard, then released. I leaned over and vomited on the polished tile. The tears came fast, unstoppable. I tried to hold them back but my body wouldn't listen. I shook as I cried, emptied, purged everything I'd locked away since Raven attacked me.

Then I heard a chuckle. "You know, you never could keep your food down." I lifted my head. Raven. She knelt beside me, her hand lifting my chin. Her fingers were ice.

"What the actual fuck? You're dead." I wanted to scream, but all I managed was a whisper. My tongue felt like cement. My limbs refused to move.

"You're right. I'm dead. You made sure of that." She cocked her head. "But not what you expected, huh?"

Her eyes were dark as coal with a flicker of something cruel beneath. I shook my head, desperate to erase the image. Like wiping an Etch A Sketch. No luck.

She stood, laughing. Hands on her hips. The same smug posture she always had when she knew she'd gotten under my skin.

"Silly girl. You'll never get rid of me. I'm all up in your head now." She jabbed a finger into my temple and cackled. "For the next few weeks, it's just you and me. Hope you're ready… Jemeka." She called me by my government name. Damn. Her heels clicked as she turned. She vanished before she reached the door.

Suddenly, I could move again. I crawled to the bathroom. Between the dry heaves, the shaking, and the tears, I collapsed. I'd killed people before—but this? This was something else. This was guilt that tasted like acid. It lived in the marrow.

Eventually, I pulled myself up. Flushed the toilet. Cleaned the foyer. Turned on the shower. The steam hit fast, heavy and comforting. I slid to the floor under the water and let it bead down my back like warm rain. The sound of the faucet was whisper soft.

My head tilted back. My eyes closed. A presence hovered above me. When I opened my eyes, Emerald was there. She looked beautiful. Peaceful. She knelt and pulled me into her arms. I clung to her. I wanted to speak, to apologize, to explain but she gently hushed me.

"Thank you for continuing to carry on," she whispered. "Nothing more needs to be said. I'm here. Always." She rocked me. Kissed the top of my head.

When the water turned cold, I knew it was time to get out. I dried myself. Found the bedroom, exactly to my specifications from the furniture to the color of the pillows. Someone had paid attention. I guess that's why I had to fill out all that paperwork.

I slid under the blankets, turning them into a cocoon, then pulled out my phone and queued my lullaby playlist. Louis Armstrong's voice filled the room. *What a Wonderful World.*

My mind drifted to better places. Better days.

Maybe tomorrow would be better.

CHAPTER 3

Return to the Fold

I pulled into a parking space and killed the engine, The silence hit harder than I expected. I leaned the seat back, closed my eyes, and let out a breath I didn't know I was holding.

Thirty days.

Too long to hide, not long enough to forget.

After the ghosts, the guilt, and the solitude, I wasn't sure what I was returning to. But the door was open; I was still breathing. That was enough—for now.

I looked at my watch and saw I had 15 minutes to meet Pearl and the new Director of Operations. Damn. I had no desire to deal with this right now. I plucked up the courage, put in my earbuds, and cranked up the music. I got out of my car and locked it. *Fuck it.* I hurried towards the main compound.

I rushed through security just to see Pearl waiting for me at the administrative desk. She must've seen my face, because she laughed. "Don't worry," she replied, "you got enough time."

She pointed towards the elevators and we marched in sync. I felt everyone's eyes follow me. I peeped my reflection in the picture and checked myself, making sure my outfit was all the way together.

A light tap on my shoulder disturbed my thoughts. "It's not your outfit. Everyone heard about your last assignment and trust, it's admiration and not condemnation." A sigh of relief escaped my lips as we hopped onto the elevator.

My mind rehashed events as we cruised to the bottom floor. The moment when my best friend, someone I considered my sister, betrayed me and my other best friend. There was a ray of light through all this: I had won. Her attempt on my life ended in her own death. It still sent chills through my spine. I didn't understand the admiration. The organization suffered a betrayal, and I neutralized the threat. The doors opened to the Director's suite. Pearl stepped in front of me and held the door handle. "Just so you know, things have changed." She opened the door to the director's suite. A young man with a boyish face and a wiry frame looked up and rose from his seat.

"Good morning, ladies. My name is Jasper, Sid's assistant. What can I do for you?"

Pearl and I exchanged looks. She narrowed her eyes at Jasper and clicked her tongue. "Is that how you address your boss in front of her subordinates?" The Air Force training instructor's voice came out like a roaring river. Instead of taking the warning, Jasper doubled down.

"Well," he rolled his eyes, "*she* is my boss, not you. If she wants me to address her as Sid, I will do so because she's my boss." He folded his arms across his chest. Pearl's knife hand came out, but I placed my hand on her arm. I knew Jasper wasn't ready for what was about to come next. Pearl lowered her hand as I stepped forward and deepened my tone of voice.

"Jasper, you need to recognize who you are addressing. Pearl is an OG; you will give her the respect she has earned and deserves. Second, it's unprofessional to address your boss in the familiar instead of the formal. You don't know us, so to assume we're cool with you is unwise. She was trying to keep you from falling off that cliff."

Jasper gulped. I heard a snicker and glanced towards the noise. Obsidian leaned against the doorway with one ankle over the other and her hands were in her pockets. Her eyebrows rose in amusement.

"Jasper." Her tongue fiddled with a toothpick in her mouth. Jasper mouthed an apology to Pearl and returned to his typing. Although Obsidian said his name and nothing else, her voice sent a shockwave through my body. And if I felt a shockwave, Jasper's pale complexion showed he felt an earthquake.

Like a dog scolded by his master, Jasper took his seat. Obsidian gave him a long, hard stare before turning her attention to us. "Ladies." She straightened her posture and spun on her heel. We scurried after her and shut her office door. She gestured to the two seats in front of her desk as she sat down.

"Don't kill him. He's still learning."

Pearl waved her hands. "Understandable."

I sucked my teeth and rolled my eyes. Obsidian stopped typing. "Something you want to say, Onyx?" Pearl turned in her seat to face my direction. I was unfazed as I shrugged.

"Don't need to explain anything for blatant disrespect. Even if he didn't know, you listen, adjust, and move accordingly." I cocked my head.

Obsidian sat back in her chair, clasped her hands above her head, and let them rest. "Make no mistake: I don't tolerate disrespect and I was about to cut him. He has you to thank for beating me to him. I'm just requesting grace on his behalf." She returned to typing as I grimaced. Maybe having an ops director like Obsidian was a great idea.

I scanned her office, noticing her office differed from Glacier's. While Glacier loved the British library vintage, Obsidian loved modern vintage with a twist. While the desk was the traditional large L-shape, it was glass instead of wood. On the walls, posters of the different naval units and ships hung proudly. Navy memorabilia were splashed everywhere. My Air Force bones shuddered at the sight.

The keyboard clacking ceased and Obsidian cleared her throat. "Ladies, I know we briefly met at the debrief, but I wanted to have a moment to meet you two. Both of you came highly recommended from Cashew. After reading the files, I have to say I'm impressed." She paused and drank her coffee before she continued. "The purpose of today's meeting is to introduce myself properly and let you know about the changes in operations. After that, there will be time for comments, questions, and/or concerns. Sound good?"

Both Pearl and I murmured our agreement. Obsidian mouthed okay and clicked a button. The wall screen rolled down and powered on. "Please direct your attention to the screen." We turned our chairs to face the screen. A slideshow appeared, and Obsidian started clicking. The next slide showed pictures of her at a deployed location in uniform.

"First, please call me Sid. Obsidian is too much, but it means the same thing. Let's be efficient." As she continued through the slides, I discovered her background was primarily intelligence and she worked with spec ops for most of her career. Glacier, Ruby, Garnet, and she were deployed together multiple times. While on active duty, she was an undercover operative for the organization. When she retired, she transitioned to here. Yep, she was a perfect fit.

"Questions so far?" Sid looked at both of us. I glanced over at Pearl, who remained stone-faced. Sid clicked her tongue and moved onto the next slide.

"Expectations: I expect communication all around, whether that's up the chain, down the chain, or across the chain. Everybody needs to be on the same page. If you need help, ask. If you need clarification, ask." She clicked on another slide and it showed an organizational chart.

"The different sections will remain the same; however, I took Pearl's suggestion and implemented teams within the different sections. Each section will have four teams, comprising of an operative, a handler, an analyst, a researcher, and a human resources rep. The HR rep will handle assignment details and will be the contact between the handler and staff members on the outside. Each section will also have a chief in charge, who will assign cases to the best qualified team."

I was excited by this new change. Usually, you received random assignments from an analyst or your handler. While my experience was different, I heard many complaints from other operatives.

Sid smiled as she continued. "Your team will be Quartz, Lotus, and Amethyst. Citrine is moving laterally and will be your new handler. She's looking forward to change and when this opportunity came up, she jumped at it." Sid paused as I felt my face scrunched up.

"I understand how you feel. Pearl is moving to be your new section chief. I knew Citrine would be a great fit for you since she was an operative and wanted to move to a handler. I figured pairing you two together would make an easier transition for you both."

I nodded my head, but I was still confused. While I was happy I still got to work with Pearl somewhat, Citrine was like a sister from another mister, and Amethyst and Lotus I knew from going through training together. I felt at ease working with such relaxed and collected individuals. But what happened to Aster? Aster was my go-to and my analyst. And who the fuck was Quartz?

Sid tossed me a couple of folders. Each folder had a team member's name on it. "Here's your team's dossier. Quartz is new and will need your guidance. He has the potential to be a brilliant analyst and maybe an operative down the road." Quartz was a dude? Great.

I blew raspberries as I grazed through the files. On the surface, it looked like a great team. Sid moved to the front of the desk and folded her arms. "Listen. I've got faith in you. You're perfect for this. If I didn't think you could pull this off, I wouldn't have done this to you. Plus, you've got Pearl and Citrine to help. Please believe me when I say this: I would never put you in a position to fail."

I closed the files and sighed. The question about Aster consumed me. I had no choice but to ask. "What about Aster? She was my go-to. Has she left or moved on?"

Sid and Pearl exchanged smiles. "Aster has been moved to Special Projects within the Nut. You'll deal with her from time to time." Hmm. Aster was still here. I nodded while Pearl and I stood up. "My team won't let you down. Thanks for the opportunity." I turned to leave.

"One more thing: have you seen Dr. Buho yet?"

Pearl spoke up for me. "She's going to see her by the end of the week."

Sid clapped her hands. "Outstanding! If there's nothing else, we're done. I'm sure you want to get ready to meet your team." She walked over to the door and opened it. I shook her hand before I left, with Pearl right behind me. Jasper glared at me as I smirked at him.

***

Pearl and I strolled down the hallway on the way to the Nut. My mind was replaying the meeting. Pearl was no longer my handler. I had a brand new team? The fuck?

Pearl cleared her throat. "I know it's a lot, and I wasn't expecting to oversee a section. If I'd known, I would've warned you."

I patted her on the shoulder. "I know. But you said things had changed."

"They told us there would be changes. I didn't know these were the changes. I knew about one which would affect you directly. But enough of that. How are you feeling?" She stopped and turned towards me.

I shrugged. "I knew you wouldn't be my permanent handler but I figured that was down the road, not now."

Pearl laughed. "Truth be told, I was in training after years of being in the field. Then moved over to being your handler and that was intense, even by my standards. I moved laterally but never up. So, I'm glad they gave me a promotion. But," she grabbed my shoulders and looked me deep in my eyes, "I want you to know I'm not abandoning you. I'm still here. Reach out if you need. Understand?"

With a grin on my face, I embraced her, the scent of her coconut, pineapple, and vanilla perfume filling my senses. I held onto her tightly. She returned the gesture. "Thank you for everything."

"No. Thank you." We did a final squeeze, wiped our eyes, and got onto the elevator.

"What happened to Jade?" I asked as the door closed. Pearl punched the floor we needed and spoke. "Jade got promoted too. She's in charge of the Peanut section. Citrine asked to be a handler since Jade moved on. Citrine said she was tired of the operative role but wanted to stay in the field. Oh my god! You should've heard her squeal once she found out her handler assignment was with you. I think since y'all are good friends already, training your team shouldn't be difficult at all."

Pearl had a point. If Pearl was no longer my handler, Citrine was the next best choice. Like me, she was fearless, but in a different type of way. Unlike Raven, Citrine balanced personal and professional business without making me feel dumb. "I agree with that assessment. But why do I have a dude on my team? We're allowing men now?"

"Men are victims, too. The leadership will still be female led, but some men will be allowed into the organization. We need to penetrate the cells and the networks they belong to, and men can help us in that regard. Also, the other positions, like the concierge, will still be available for men."

I thought about Quartz joining my team and then I remembered Raccoon. Although he was a horrible friend to me, he was still a victim. And no one can accomplish great things alone. You still need people to help you get there, no matter the background.

The conversation got too heavy for my taste, so I changed the subject. "What's on the agenda for today?"

"Going to see the new digs and then I'll brief you on what you and Citrine need to do." The elevator doors opened and Pearl cocked her head towards her new office. It was modest, but I assumed Pearl would upgrade it later, given her promotion. She closed the door and locked it. Pearl pointed to a chair, and she took the seat right next to me.

Pearl spoke in a hushed tone. "What I'm about to tell you must stay here. Swear it."

I gulped while trying to still be calm. "Even Citrine?"

Pearl shook her head. "For Citrine, not yet."

I removed my tiger eye and onyx bracelet and placed it on her desk. "You have my word." Pearl took off her own pearl and diamond bracelet and placed her and mine into a stoneware bowl. She took some drops of sage and cinnamon oil and rubbed the mixture onto the gems. She took the bowl and placed it in a drawer, then closed and locked the drawer.

"You are to meet Aster in the Server room right after this meeting. Please be discreet. She'll explain everything. Please know that whatever Aster tells you, it must be kept to yourself. The only ones who will know are me, Glacier, Sid, and Garnet. After she briefs you, you will get with Citrine in the Cashew section and go over your team's information."

"Understood." I rose from my chair and walked towards the door. By now, if Pearl told me something secret and sacred, I obeyed.

"Oh," Pearl said as my hand touched the knob, "your appointment with Dr. Buho is tomorrow at 1400. You'll arrive 30 minutes early." She grinned as she typed on her phone.

My jaw dropped. "When did you have time to do that?"

"While Sid was talking to you about her background. I figured you hadn't made an appointment yet and you were so enamored by her resume, I decided you could tell Dr. Buho all about it."

I shook my head and gave her a small salute. She saluted back, and I walked out to meet Aster. My heart felt heavy, excited, and secure all at once. One thing for sure: Pearl would always have my back, no matter what.

CHAPTER 4

Where Ghosts Don't Follow

The combination of the server hums, the dark room, and the illuminated floors felt as if something sinister was in the air. My mind was playing tricks on me. I wondered why I was meeting Aster here. Usually, I met her in a conference room. This was different. Special projects? What the hell did that mean? I kept coming up with answers to that question until I heard a clear ahem. I whirled around and saw Aster emerge from behind one of the servers.

"Damn! Where the hell you come from?" I tried to hide the tremble of my voice as I grabbed my chest and let out a huge sigh of relief. Aster grabbed and squeezed me tight. Then, she gave me a casual slap on the shoulder.

"Hey! It's the legend herself! Welcome back!"

I sucked my teeth. I looked around as if searching for someone. Legend? Where? Very laughable, indeed.

She must've read my face because she snickered. "Look. You took down the traitor at personal cost. You're definitely a legend, whether you believe it or not. And it's not up for debate, especially from you."

My body suddenly felt lighter. I needed to hear that from someone other than my bosses. Bosses tell you about things hoping you move past the traumatic event and keep doing the job to the same or higher level. Hearing it from a friendly colleague let me know I did the right thing. I gave her another hug and closed my eyes. This moment seemed to last just long enough for me to regain a piece of my former self. I opened my eyes and Raven's snarling face flashed in the darkness. Would that girl ever leave me alone?

"Why are the lights off?" I whispered in Aster's ear as I scanned the room.

She giggled. "We got to keep the servers cool. Anyway, glad you're down here 'cause I got something to show you!" She grabbed my hand and dragged me to another room. I scrambled to keep up with her, her energy like a kid tearing down the stairs on Christmas morning.

We stopped in front of a door resembling a bank vault with a cyber lock. I panted as Aster punched in her code and had her eye scanned to gain access. The door hissed as it unlocked, and she beckoned me to follow her.

My eyes adjusted to the lighting as we walked in. She plopped down in a seat and pulled up another one. I eased into the chair and wondered why this room looked like a recording booth.

"So, are we going to record a demo?" I twisted in my chair and looked around.

Aster's light-hearted laugh filled the space. She pushed a button, changing the lighting to a soft arctic blue. What was she setting the mood for? I squinted my eyes as she turned away from the control panel. Her smile diminished into a brooding line.

"Do you remember the conversation we had about changing the current ops? You said you wished I was with you on your missions so I could give you real time analysis?"

I nodded my head, vividly recalling the mission where Aster was on speed dial about some info I needed. Her information and timeliness proved crucial to my mission's success.

She leaned in closer as if she had a secret. "What if I made it a possibility for you?"

I cocked my head to side, curiosity rising.

A soft cough escaped Aster's throat. Her eyes shimmered in the arctic light—pride flickering there but shadowed by something unspoken.

She handed me a small keychain. "Push the middle button and hold it for 3 seconds. Once you see the yellow lights, introduce yourself loud and clear." Aster sat back with her fingers entwined. I shrugged and did as I was commanded.

"Hello, this is Onyx." The device vibrated in my palm. A strangely lifelike female voice, calm in tone, filled the room.

"Hello, Onyx. It's so nice to finally meet you."

My arm hairs stood up as shivers were sent down my spine. Whoa! What the fuck? Who the fuck? The lights on the device turned blue.

Aster grinned, but her fingers tapped against the chair. "Onyx, meet the next best thing to me. Meet your personal analyst."

I froze, still staring at the keychain like it might sprout legs. My brows pulled together, and I tilted my head—half awe, half suspicion.

"She doesn't see, if that's what you're wondering," Aster added, almost reading my thoughts. "Crystal builds a full picture from data — environmental sensors, heat readings, sound frequencies, even your own pulse. What you'll perceive from her isn't sight, it's translation. Think of it as intelligence stitched together from everything around you."

My eyes widened, and my jaw dropped. I gulped as I tried to regain my composure. What exactly was this? Whatever it was, Aster is very talented.

Aster twirled in her chair as she spread her arms. "This is Special Projects. Think of it as the Q branch of Mi6. After the developments from your last mission and your feedback, I wanted to create an entity you can take everywhere and only you would know…unless you tell somebody."

Incredible. Simply incredible. I felt my face turn warm as my lips crept to the corners of my ears. "I didn't even know you knew how to program or create anything like this."

Aster shrugged and waved me off. "Which is why it's top secret. I was able to create, develop, and program her without anyone noticing. It was nice not being pinged for months."

I couldn't contain the butterflies anymore. "When can I test it out?"

The humanlike voice answered. "I'm here with you all the time. As soon as you activated me, I was able to adapt and continue to adapt to your needs. Just say the word."

"Word." I suppressed a laugh.

"Ah. I see a sense of humor. Noted."

Aster and I chuckled. "She already knows me so well." I muttered as I stood up and folded my arms. "So, what do I call you? I mean if we're gonna be working together, we should be on a first name basis."

"That's up to you. I'm just technology after all. Just be respectful, please."

"Technology with manners? Clever and interesting." That was a good question. What would her name be? And at least she said please. Suddenly, I was Sir Isaac Newton after the apple clunked me on the head.

"I need you to be open, honest, and clear with me," I said. "And you are essentially a part of this organization. Therefore, I shall name you…Crystal."

A pregnant silence filled the room. Aster's eyebrows rose in approval.

"Hmm," Crystal said. "That's a lot better than I thought. I was expecting something like Windex or Saran Wrap."

I burst out laughing. "Oh yeah, we're going to get along so well." I turned to Aster. "So, does Crystal turn off or how do I call her when I need her?"

Aster rolled her eyes. "Have you ever watched any shows like Star Trek? You ask, she answers. The only thing though, is to always keep the keychain on you. It's also digitally imprinted so no one can access Crystal but you."

"Awesome. Is she standard issue or…?"

"If you're asking if everyone has one, no. You're the only one. We wanted you to test it first since Crystal came from your inputs and suggestions. Also," she stepped closer and whispered, "only Glacier, Sid, Pearl, and I know about Crystal. Keep her to yourself unless otherwise instructed."

I gave a thumbs up sign. The positive energy rumbled through my body until I realized I wouldn't be working with Aster anymore. The high crashed like a sudden urge to use the bathroom.

"Onyx. I detected a plummet in your mood. Want to talk about it?"

"Crystal. I just met you. Let's take baby steps."

"Understood. I'm sure you'd rather talk to Dr. Buho anyway as you have an appointment with her after this."

"I noticed sarcasm and eye rolling from you, Crystal."

"How can I roll something I don't have?"

I frowned. Aster shook her head and placed her hand on my shoulder. "I noticed it too. What's up?"

I sighed, my shoulders slumped under the weight of my frustration and grief. "I just realized we aren't working together anymore. Is this the end?"

"Not at all. It's more of a 'see you later'. I'll check in from time to time to see how you two are getting along but I fear there won't be any problems."

We embraced as if we knew this might be the last time we would see each other. Aster smoothed her hair. "Whelp, you and Crystal have fun. If I know you, you already got plans for her."

"You know I do." I cracked my neck and knuckles. "Ready, Crystal?"

"Let's do this."

"Don't worry, Crystal. Onyx will take good care of you. Just make sure you take care of her. She's gonna need you."

"Will do. And yeah, I gathered that after 15 minutes of meeting her."

Aster looked at me as she rolled her eyes. "She's all yours. If you need help, let me know. You got my number."

I nodded as I turned to leave. "See you soon, Aster."

"Time will tell, Legend."

I smiled as I left the room. Aster will be missed.

"I know you miss her, but don't worry. I'm here for your analytical and sound boarding needs."

"I appreciate that, Crystal." I wiped my eyes as I took a deep breath. "C'mon. Let's go analyze my team and see what we're dealing with."

"Excellent. Sounds like a plan."

I closed the door behind me as I hurried out of the server room. Crystal and I had work to do.

CHAPTER 5

Assembly

I commandeered a secure meeting room to review the dossier on my team. The dim lighting and closed door added to my sense of security—and comfort. I pulled the keychain from my pocket and placed it on the table. It emanated a soft glow, setting the tone for the room.

Hours passed in silence as I perused. My finger swiped lightly against the screen while I sighed between thoughts. To her credit, Crystal stood by, letting me settle into a rhythm that might build trust. Confidence.

"For the love of everything that's holy," I muttered, staring at the files on my tablet. "Where should I begin?"

On cue, Crystal's voice pierced the quiet, calm and smooth.

"I would suggest at the beginning. What you want to know the most should be priority. I've processed their files. Would you like tactical summaries, emotional profiles, predicted group cohesion... or all the above?"

I stared up at the ceiling. "I was wondering when you were gonna show up."

"I was giving you space. Didn't want to just jump in. You seem like the type who doesn't like that."

I chuckled. "Very perceptive of you. How about we start with a summary that includes everything?"

"Acknowledges observations. Likes straightforward data. Needs all angles before making a decision. This is very wise."

That compliment hit deeper than I expected. "Thanks. I appreciate that." I shifted forward in my chair. "Now let's see what we've got. Who's up first?"

"Does the order matter?"

"Surprise me, Crystal."

"Alright. Up first: the rookie on the all-star team—Quartz."

I blinked. "Hold up. Did you just quote Lil' Kim?"

"Technically, Angie Martinez on a song spearheaded by Lil' Kim."

I snorted. "I stand corrected. As you were."

"Thank you. Anyway, Quartz is an orange/gold mix: practical, loyal, aware of the rules but prone to pushing limits. Highly intelligent. Adaptable. Fast problem solver. He fights when he feels underestimated—but give him a chance to prove himself and he'll seize it. Just... keep an eye on the recklessness. He's got something to prove."

I studied his photo. So young. But behind his eyes—dark clouds. Ominous ones.

"You see something?" Crystal asked.

"Damn. You psychic now?"

"Not psychic. But based on your breath rate, lower vocal tone, and the fact you didn't deflect with a quip—yes, I can tell something's bothering you."

"Just skeptical. He's young. And I have trust issues… especially when it comes to guys. One of the reasons I joined this organization. Now we're recruiting them. Hm. Wonder what his story is."

"You'll have the chance to ask him. And youth and gender doesn't dictate experience."

Crystal was getting a little too comfortable. "Let's be clear—you're a tool. A smart one. But still a tool."

"Understood. But tools protect their operators."

Damn. That hit harder than I expected.

"I get it," I muttered. "But don't analyze me unless I ask."

"Noted. But for the record—I wasn't analyzing. Just acknowledging the weight of the grief you carry. You carry it in your silence."

I was speechless. Crystal hadn't even been here long and already she saw me more clearly than most ever had.

A cough helped clear my throat. "Please introduce the next member?"

"Next is Lotus. Blue surrounds her—empathy, calm, high EQ. Former linguistic and cultural analyst. Now serves as your team's researcher. Detail-oriented. Patient. Spiritual."

I drummed my fingers on the table. She could balance out Quartz. Not a bad pairing.

"Alright. Hope she doesn't mind me cursing."

"Probably light a candle and throw some holy water on you. You might feel some burning."

I laughed. "Okay, that was actually good. Keep going. Who's next?"

"My pleasure. Up next—Amethyst. The green one. Logical, efficient, by the book. Former operative reassigned to HR after burnout. Zero red flags. High processing power. Tactical HR, if such a thing exists."

I squinted my eyes as I stared at her picture. I heard tales about her from Raven. She had no filter when it came to her mouth. And word on the street was that she beat her old commander with a baseball bat. She might be a difficult colleague, or she could be invaluable, uniting the team with her decisive approach. The jury was still out.

I took a breath. "So, I've got a priest, a cowboy, and a green beret. What a cast."

"Or… a library, a computer, and a car. Depends on how you lead them."

I powered off the tablet and leaned back in the chair. "And how am I gonna do this?"

"With the same grace, wisdom, and skill you used on past missions. Or you can crash and burn. Entirely up to you."

"Comforting."

"I need your respect. I won't lie to you."

"As you shouldn't." I stood, stretching. "I'm calling it a night. Meeting Citrine in the morning. Team in the afternoon."

"Sounds like a plan. Anything else?"

"One more thing—do you have an off switch?"

"Oh yeah. Aster failed to mention this. To put me in sleep mode, say: 'Good night, Crystal.' To wake me: 'Good morning, Crystal.' I'll pick up right where we left off."

Clever girl, Aster. "Well then. Good night, Crystal."

"Good night, Commander. Good job today." The glow from the keychain changed from blue to red.

Out of curiosity, I whispered, "Crystal?"

Silence.

Following her lead, I made my way to the parking lot and drove home.

***

After an uneventful evening and morning without any ghosts, I had a light breakfast and completed a workout at my condo's gym to get my mind right. I arrived at work, mentally preparing myself for the day. To help me prepare, I decided to wake up Crystal.

"Good morning, Crystal." A slight vibration rumbled from the key fob as the lights changed from crimson to cerulean.

"Good morning, Commander. How's your day going so far?"

"Can't complain too much."

"If you did, it would change anything."

I chuckled at the truth.

Crystal's voice changed from playful to concern. "Take some deep breaths. It will help lower your heart rate."

I brushed it off and sipped on some water instead. The cool liquid replenished my insides and helped clear out some of the cobwebs in my head.

"I guess you could've done that too to get the same result." Crystal quipped.

"You will learn I like to do things my way sometimes. Nothing against your suggestion but I'm tired of everyone telling me to take deep breaths. There are other ways to get the same result."

"Noted. I will adapt. Now, just as a suggestion, would you like for me to tell you about your itinerary for today or would you rather wing it?"

Smart ass. I sighed. "Why don't you tell me so we're on the same page?"

"So, you've got a meeting with Citrine in thirty minutes, then you're meeting with the team, followed by an out brief with Pearl. The last appointment of the day is with Dr. Buho at 1400."

Ugh. I rolled my eyes. "Do you think I could skip Dr. Buho? Or reschedule for another day?"

"Protocol dictates after each operation/assignment, the team must attend one counseling session with one of the company's therapists. You've put this off for 30 days AND you are on the naughty list, my friend."

I was taken aback. "Naughty list? There's a naughty list?"

"Of course there's a naughty list."

I lowered my tone even though I was the only one in the car. "Can you tell me who else is on the naughty list?"

"Commander. I can only tell you what's in your record."

I had to pry. "Not even a hint?"

"Nope. It's against my code of ethics."

"Speaking of, what are your limitations? What can't you do?"

A pause hung in the air for about ten seconds.

"I can't go into other people's records unless they are part of the team AND it's mission related. I'm not able to discuss any of our conversations unless you're going to harm yourself and others who aren't on the target list."

"Hmm. That's not bad and it leaves us open to communicate and execute freely."

"Not quite, but enough."

"I'll try not to break your trust."

"I know you won't, Commander."

She called me that name again. I liked the way it sounded and my curiosity was piqued.

"What's the reason behind the 'Commander' moniker?"

As if waiting for me to ask, she answered without skipping a beat. "That's what you are right now. You're commanding a team. Might as well get used to it."

I beamed. "You're amazing."

"I only reflect the brilliance of my owner. It's time to meet with Citrine. Ready, Commander?"

"As I'll ever be." I got out of my car and locked the door. Taking a deep breath, I strutted towards my first appointment of the day, bursting with confidence and optimism.

***

After clearing security, I stepped into the elevator and pressed the button for the Nut—the nerve center of the entire organization. As the elevator descended, it hit me: I had no idea where Citrine was.

"Hey Crystal," I murmured. "Where's Citrine located?"

"She's in Meeting Room Two," Crystal replied smoothly, her voice soft in the enclosed space. "A little ways past Pearl's office. Estimated time of arrival: five minutes."

"Also… how am I supposed to talk to you in front of people?"

"Remove the center piece of your key fob and place it in your ear. That way only you hear my voice."

I pressed the center button. It popped out like a capsule—sleek, discreet, shaped like an earbud. I slid it in. It fit like a hand in a glove. Perfect.

"Thanks," I whispered, just as the elevator chimed and the doors parted.

I stepped out, greeting the familiar faces I passed, trying to shake off the creeping weight of self-doubt. As if sensing it, Crystal's voice whispered again.

"Relax, Commander."

I nodded slightly, taking that in. The title still felt strange on my skin—but I wore it anyway.

When I opened the door to Meeting Room Two, warm amber light bathed the space. Five desks were arranged in a semi-circle around a main station facing the door. Each had its own laptop dock, power station, and small lamp. On the main desk, Citrine sat hunched over her laptop, sipping from a wide ceramic mug, brow furrowed in concentration.

I coughed gently. "Look at you—beat me here! All early and shit."

Citrine looked up and grinned, her teeth gleaming like pearls, her New Orleans drawl rolling in like a Sunday brass band. "Welcome home, baby! Looking sharp as always. Oohh… and look at that hair! The majesty!" She stood up and rushed over, arms wide. That warm, electric energy of hers—unmistakable.

She hugged me tight before guiding me to a seat beside her, still glowing.

"Man, I'm so excited for this!" she said, practically bouncing. "Remember we talked about this back in Utrecht? Didn't think it would happen so soon!"

"Same. I thought we'd do a little collab first—then maybe something permanent. But I guess there were plans beyond us. Worked out either way."

We high-fived and shared a few minutes of easy laughter before diving into the real conversation. As Citrine told me about her transition, I drifted back to that memory—her and Wilhelm, warning me about Raven. She'd never been one to keep her cards close. Citrine laid it all out, no filter, and still got shit done. She was perfect for this role.

"Anyway," she went on, "I wanted a change. Jade got promoted and I wasn't about to be assigned to another handler. I asked to step into handler duties and boom—this gig opened up. I jumped."

She hesitated. "I hope you weren't too close to Pearl?"

"Nah. Pearl got promoted, and I'm happy for her. She was always meant to move on. Besides, she was just temporary. I was kind of prepared."

Citrine sighed in relief. "Good! I was nervous about that."

She cleared her throat and pushed a folder toward me. "Let's get to business. I figured you'd want notes with the files."

I flipped through her notes, nodding. They echoed my thoughts exactly: strong individual skill sets, but green as a team. With guidance, though? They'd be a force.

Citrine gave me a moment. "Initial thoughts?"

I closed the folder. "We're aligned. But looks like I'll have to play bad cop for a while."

Citrine winced playfully. "Or not. Show them respect, and you'll earn it right back."

I shifted in my chair. "You know how I come off. My tone. My face."

She reached out and took my hands. "You're not going to knock it out of the park on day one. No one does. But you've got the strength to lead them. Just like they'll grow—you'll grow. They'll adapt to you, and you to them. You've got this. Stop acting scary and lead."

I gulped down a bottle of water. The cold jolted me back into the moment.

Crystal's voice whispered in my ear again. "Your team, minus Quartz, is en route. ETA: eight minutes."

Since I couldn't exactly explain that, I glanced at Citrine. "Everyone on their way?"

"All but Quartz. You'll meet him later. The others are almost here."

I exhaled and began smoothing the hem of my sleeve, adjusting my hair in a moment of silent nerves. Citrine noticed. She placed a firm hand on my arm.

"Look at me."

I did.

"How are you, really?"

I shrugged. "I'm managing." Kind of the truth.

Citrine narrowed her eyes. "The bones don't lie. If we're a true partnership, you gotta share the secrets. Just like the bones do."

I nodded just as her gaze flicked to the door.

"They've arrived," she whispered.

The door blew open and Amethyst strode into the room with Lotus behind her closing the door. Amethyst nodded her head towards me and Citrine while Lotus smiled her hellos. Amethyst immediately took the desk closest to me while setting up her laptop. Lotus took the seat closest to the rear, setting up her diffuser and iced bottle of lemon water.

I glanced over to Citrine as she gave me a slight nod, encouraging me to start the meeting.

"Morning, ladies. I'm Onyx and this here is Citrine. We wanted to meet with y'all since we're going to be a team. Before moving forward, I wanted to get to know y'all outside of the files I've read and meet the real person. You can introduce yourself however you wish, but please know you were chosen to be a part of the team for your specific skill set." I paused to make sure I had everyone's attention. Amethyst was typing what I assumed were notes while Lotus sat straight in her chair, hands enfolded.

"We won't be cohesive overnight; no great team is. But we have the potential to become a force to be reckoned with. To do that, what do y'all need from me to accomplish this?"

The clicking on the keyboard stopped and Amethyst's eyes met mine. Her glare shot through me—not hateful, but sharp, with purpose.

"I've been where you were and I know how difficult it can be. My main concern is chain of command. Sometimes, you hear from the handler and sometimes the analyst and then a researcher would chime in. It was confusing at best."

I agreed, remembering how I received my assignment. Sometimes, I receive my assignments from other field agents. That flight attendant I met on my first mission? She was another agent. Hell, my plane tickets were given to me via email. If I wanted updates, I had to reach out to an analyst and it usually wasn't the same analyst. I understood her pain.

"You're right, it's chaotic and doesn't help the operative at all. If anything, it hinders progress and trust, which ultimately hinders success. What do you think?"

Her eyes widened as her aura changed from dark to light. She spun her laptop so it faced me and Citrine. Citrine held her hand up and held up a remote. "Wait a minute; connect your laptop to the big screen so all of us can see."

Amethyst grabbed the remote and connected. The screen flickered and then showed a flow chart complete with time expectations and departments.

"See, if Quartz and Lotus work together, while I deal with the logistics such as weapons, travel details, locations, etc. Then, we present our products to Citrine, who will put the finishing touches and give you the entire package, which should consist of everything you need to get the mission done."

I stroked my chin in thought. Ugh, I need a chin wax soon. "Is this for normal ops? If so, this setup will work. For abnormal ops, I or Citrine should be able to reach the specific person directly."

Amethyst raised her hands. "Oh, I understand and agree. I just think we all need to be on the same page. One band, one sound."

Lotus's hand inches up towards the sky. Damn, she's so quiet. "What's up, Lotus?"

Her voice barely raised above a whisper. I had to strain just to hear her. "This seems like a good chain of command. But I have two concerns. One, will I have all access to files, including archives if it is associated with a case? And two, will we be called upon to do other cases from other department? Sometimes I find myself juggling multiple cases from different departments in the Archives department all at once."

I leaned back in my chair as if I was hit with some electrical current. "Damn! How'd you keep up with the demand?"

She grinned, her face brightening. "By prioritizing. I knew which departments required immediate attention, like Cashew and Peanut. Cold cases, unless connected to an ongoing case, usually went last. Using this method, I was able to clear my caseload efficiently and still look good." She fluffed her hair.

Citrine snapped her fingers while I brushed some dirt off my shoulder.

"I'm impressed. Let's address your concerns. You are assigned to one department, one team. Unless it comes from Pearl or Sid, your focus is on our team's assigned cases. If you run into any interference, let me and Citrine know. Trust, between the two of us, we'll either get you access or have an answer as to why you won't get access."

Lotus did a little dance in her seat. I guess my answer satisfied her.

A sense of pride and excitement swelled inside of me. I glanced at my right hand, waiting to see if she had anything to add.

On cue, Citrine picked up where I left off. "We'll get together again but next time it'll be with Quartz. He's active-duty so he couldn't get away like us veterans."

A light laugh was shared. I was thankful she addressed the lingering question about Quartz.

She scanned the room to see if anyone else had anything before continuing. "If there's nothing else, we'll see you tomorrow when we get our first assignment."

We stood up and shook hands, trading a few affirmations and nods. The energy in this group was electric. As soon as the other two left, Citrine closed the door, her eyebrows raised as she plopped into her seat.

"Before we brief Pearl, what are your thoughts on our crew?"

I closed my eyes and let my head roll back. That stretch in my neck felt amazing. "Both are self-sufficient, which is a strength. Luckily for me, I won't have to babysit but I can foresee issues arising. Won't really know until we meet with Quartz and see them interact together."

I opened my eyes and turned to her. "What about you?"

"I liked how you told them the protocol of them giving me their products and I give a quality control check before giving you the package. I also liked her saying: one band, one sound. Somehow, it resonates."

I stood up to stretch my legs. Crystal spoke as soon as I checked my watch. "You've got a meeting with Pearl in about six minutes. If you leave now, you'll be on time."

"Citrine," I took a sip of water. "What time's our meeting with Pearl?"

Citrine cursed. "Shit! We got five minutes! Ready?"

I scooped up the files and exhaled. I walked over to the door and opened it. "Let's do it."

$$* * *$$

We arrived at Pearl's office with seconds to spare. As we caught our breath outside Pearl's door, I was surprisingly calm. This was the first time I'd interacted with Pearl in her new role, but something about this felt familiar. I did a little shimmy to shake off the nerves and tapped on the door. Citrine was beside me, shuffling through her notes and breathing heavily. I placed my hand on her shoulder. "Relax," I mouthed to her. She nodded and took in some deep breaths. The confident Citrine I knew and loved returned.

Just then, we heard a beep and a click. I looked down at the door handle and noticed there was a green light on top. I guessed it meant we could go in. I opened the door and saw Pearl standing by her bookshelf, setting up books and pictures. She spun around and gestured towards two seats in front of her desk. We quickly sat down and Pearl leaned against her desk in front of us, arms folded across her chest as she stared at the ground.

"Give it to me whiskey straight," Pearl started, "what are we thinking?"

I crossed my legs. "On paper, the team looks great. The make up on this team is strong considering everyone's skill set. In person, they match what's on paper. Don't know about Quartz yet since he wasn't there. We'll see."

Citrine chimed in, her voice steady. "Agreed. Until we see them in a real-world situation, we can't give you an accurate assessment."

Pearl twisted her body and grabbed a file off her desk. She tossed it to me and Citrine. "Here's your chance."

I narrowed my eyes as I leaned in with Citrine and looked over the dossier. Pearl gave us a minute before she pressed.

"This is a low-level assignment. Just some scout work. Quartz is currently undercover on this one as it pertains to his unit. That bit of information stays here."

I lifted my head and noticed her face was stone. "There's a trafficking ring and we suspect Quartz's unit is involved. We just need more information on the whereabouts and what's going on. We got names of some of the major players, but we need some experts on this."

I leaned back in my chair. "So that's it? Just doing some eavesdropping?"

Pearl leaned in. "I'm not going to throw your team to the wolves when you haven't even worked together yet." She leaned back and her voice returned to normal.

"Citrine, do the others trust y'all yet?"

"I think so."

"You think, or you know?" Damn, Pearl.

Citrine straightened up in the chair. "After answering questions about the chain of command and various methods to capture the information needed for mission success, I know they trust we have their back." Damn. I felt like I was at a tennis match.

Pearl smirked. "Glad to hear it. Onyx." My head snapped to attention. "One more thing: you two are my best assets. I know y'all won't fuck up this assignment. I want an update on this case no later than midweek next. Understood?"

I acknowledged her words while grabbing the dossier and stood up. Citrine followed my lead.

"We won't disappoint."

"I know." Pearl's tone sat on my chest.

So much was said without saying it. My shoulders felt heavy. Citrine and I walked out of Pearl's office, discussing our next moves.

"I'll contact the team to meet us in room 2. We can divide tasks and update them on deadlines."

"Sounds like a plan." I stopped in front of the restroom. I really had to go. Citrine must've seen my dance because she giggled. "I won't hold you."

I told her thanks and then an idea popped into my head. *One band, one sound.* That statement stayed on repeat in my head. We weren't just building a team; we were creating a rhythm. I stopped and turned around. "How about naming Room 2 the Music Room? One band, one sound?"

Citrine tilted her head, the wheels turning. "I actually like it." My two-step dance was getting intense. "Go ahead and go. I'll see you there."

I made a dash to the first available toilet. As I emptied my bladder, two thoughts appeared: 1. I hope there's toilet paper; and 2. I hope I don't fuck this up.

CHAPTER 6

Target Shift

The plaza downtown seemed alive considering it was only Wednesday. I was on a date for the first time in three years. I was ready to get to know this gorgeous man I picked up from the gym a little bit better.

I crossed the plaza, scanning the crowd out of habit. Crystal was already online, but I needed her presence to be minimal for the time being.

"Hey, Crystal?"

"Yes, Commander?"

"I need you to be in silent mode for this evening. Alert me on any anomalies."

"Understood." A buzz indicated a switch to surveillance mode. This was supposed to be a date, not recon; but I'd learned long ago that one could turn into the other.

Paul caught my eye while I worked on my third set of lat pull-downs. He helped me with my form and I couldn't help but give him my phone number. Paul was built like a tall brick wall: sturdy and tough. Even with the rough exterior, he had the most mesmerizing hazel eyes. Those eyes would captivate a woman's soul with their mystery, danger, and touch of gentleness. After flirting for two weeks, we decided to set a date for dinner at one of the hottest restaurants in the city.

After parking my car, I checked my appearance one last time. My hair styled in loose curls while my makeup was minimal, highlighting my lips and eyes. Yep, definitely getting some tonight.

I was standing in front of a store window when I heard a low husky voice mingled with a musky vanilla scent.

"So glad I decided to dress appropriately." The faint scent of masculinity beckoned me to turn around. Damn, those eyes. To quiet the urge to pounce and devour him, I smiled. "Hey! It's great to see you. You look amazing!" I was careful not to let him know I examined him up and down – dressed and undressed. I could tell by his suit he had it tailored; each piece of fabric immaculately hugged his body.

Paul kissed my forehead and grabbed my hand. We walked toward the restaurant as if we owned the world. As we chatted, I analyzed his appearance. The perfect fit of his suit suggested he was a control freak and knew how to get what he wanted. Even on my off time, I was working.

Restaurant Ember had a dark, mysterious vibe that instantly pulled you into its environment. The atmosphere matched our outfits and moods seamlessly. I could feel my inner goddess stir, ready to explore. The rounds of smoked libations, the delectable appetizers, and the luscious entrees were designed to awaken anybody's desire to explore each other's taboos. With our drinks and food ordered, Paul turned his attention to me. I could tell he studied me while I talked about my military service and my high school experiences – not just my body language, but also my words. It seemed as if he tried to penetrate my entire being. As he sipped his whiskey neat, his smoldering eyes lit a fire in me so hot I was afraid I wouldn't be able to contain it. Before the fire became out of control, I excused myself and went to the bathroom. I rushed over to the sink and doused a paper towel in cold water. I patted my neck and face and felt instant relief. I took deep breaths as I counted to ten. Once I calmed down, I knew I wanted to take him home.

I returned to the table and noticed he unfastened the top two buttons on his shirt, showing a sliver of toned chest. He licked his lips and leaned back in his chair. "Everything alright?" His lips curled in a wicked grin.

"Yeah, just had to use the bathroom. Thanks for asking." I had to play it polite, or I would have reached over that table, bit his lip, and sucked his tongue just to taste him.

"No worries. Did you want to get out of here and go somewhere else? I know a grown and sexy party that's happening down the street. Want to go?" I swear I could hear the glistening chime from his teeth when he smiled.

My phone rang when I was about to answer his question. *Meet me in 20 minutes.* Attached was a pinned location. Seriously, Citrine had great timing and damn, I really didn't want to leave Paul and goddamn! She only gave me twenty minutes?! Doesn't anybody value the fact that I hate being rushed? But duty calls.

"Everything ok?" His head cocked to the side with his eyebrows furrowed.

"Yeah, my firm just pinged me. We're working on a major case, and I guess there's a break. Unfortunately, I've got to call it a night." I sighed as I reached for my purse.

"Understandable. How about lunch next week when you got the time? We can discuss your case and finish what we started."

Those lips looked so delicious.

"I'll take you up on that offer. I hate to leave things unfinished." I stood up and smoothed down my dress. After he paid for our dinner, he walked me outside. I profusely apologized and promised to make it up. He laughed and said he couldn't wait to hear the outcome of the case. I reached up and kissed Paul good night on his cheek. I couldn't do his mouth because it would have led to some other things I didn't have time to indulge in. We waved our good-byes and I headed up the street to meet Citrine.

The location was right around the corner and up the block. It wasn't a long distance, but in heels, it might as well have been. I don't know where Citrine just came from, but she looked amazing with her high ponytail and a backless jumpsuit. She looked up from her phone and smiled.

"We found our target." Citrine spun on her heel and started to walk forward up the block.

"Already?" My mind and body instantly switched from freak mode to operative mode. I walked beside her and put my hair up in a bun.

"He lives in the city; it wasn't hard to find him 'cause he wasn't hiding. There's a party going on tonight downtown at an undisclosed location. I got us two tickets; we'll confront him there."

Citrine started to speed walk, turning her attention back to her phone. I felt a buzz in my purse. I was about to pull out my phone until Citrine put her hand on mine. The small gesture reminded me we were in the street and didn't want to draw attention to myself in case someone was watching.

"Remember, we're just going to talk to him, nothing more."

"Hold up. Didn't I read in his file somewhere about his violent behavior? It may get a little messy if he comes out of pocket." I picked up the pace to keep up with Citrine while trying not to run out of breath. Damn, my heels were killing me.

"I've seen your handiwork. You've seen mine. Not too worried about that part." She shrugged her shoulders as her pace quickened.

By now, it felt as if we were sprinting. I placed my hand on her shoulder and stopped. "Hey, since we're walking, can't we change shoes or something? You know, something with a flat heel, perhaps?" I smiled at her while pleading with my eyes.

"Already arranged. We're here." I looked to my side and saw we were in front of a shoe store. The display of heels, sneakers, flats, and leather accessories called my name. As we walked through the door, I made a mental note to come back here and scoop me a pair or two.

While Citrine and Myrtle, the owner of the store, exchanged pleasantries, I removed my phone from my purse. Citrine just sent me the portfolio on our person of interest. While I scanned the picture and the documents, my eyes spied on a beautiful pair of inky blue-black sneakers. I put my phone back in my purse, whistled low, grabbed them off the display, and brushed my hand against the supple leather. I'm such a sucker for a good shoe and this was museum quality. From toe to heel, the shoe felt like butter. The leather had a rich tobacco and whiskey smell. I almost forgot where I was when Citrine cleared her throat.

"Look, I know how much you love your shoes but we got business to take care of. Stay focused." Citrine gave me the sister look. Like a sullen child, I groaned and pouted as I put the shoes back on display and followed her and Myrtle to a small room at the back of the store.

Once the door closed and introductions were made, Myrtle addressed me in a professional yet motherly tone. "I see you loved the black sneakers." The light in her eyes jumped in delight as she told me about how she saw the admiration I had for those sneakers.

"Oh yes, they're exquisite," I gushed as my mind trailed off to the moment I felt the leather in my hands for the first time. Myrtle walked over to a counter and grabbed a shoe box. She sauntered back as if she was walking down a high fashion runway.

"Try them on," she commanded as she handed me the box.

I hid my excitement as I obediently slipped my feet into the shoes. Oh. My. God. These shoes felt as good as they looked. I rolled through my mind as I tried to remember how much I had in my bank account to pay for these slices of heaven presently on my feet. I walked around testing the shoes while Myrtle stood back with arms crossed and beamed. Citrine smirked and kept looking at her phone.

"Citrine contacted me in advance. These shoes are also pre-treated so they will always look new AND they have a lifetime guarantee. You're going to need them for tonight."

My jaw dropped to the floor. I struggled to speak clearly. "H-h-h-how much?"

"Complete the assignment and leave a five-star review on my website and we'll call it even."

I agreed as I put my stilettos in the sneaker box. I started to do calf raises and heel flexors to try out my new sneakers. Whew, my feet felt so much better. I turned around and saw a full-length mirror propped against the wall. I spun like a dreidel, admiring my entire outfit complete with my dream shoes.

"Onyx, quit looking in the mirror and get over here." Citrine's voice snapped me out of my cloud. I took a final twirl in the mirror before I walked over to the table where Citrine and a young man who wasn't there previously scoured over the papers and photos spread across the table. I took my place beside her and looked over the documents. Man, these shoes were like butter.

Citrine glanced up at me and gestured towards the young man. "Meet Quartz. He's going to be our tour guide for tonight. He's done extensive research into this case." I took one look at Quartz and wondered if it was past his bedtime. He grinned at me as if he read my mind and tilted his chin up.

"Hey. I'm Quartz but you can call me Q. In the actual world, I'm Army Sergeant Omar Jackson, currently stationed here. I'm 26 years old even though I look as if I just graduated high school." He stuck out his hand to shake mine and I grabbed it. He gave off little brother vibes – cute but in an awkward and cheesy way.

"Nice to meet you. What we got going on here?" I switched back to business mode as I felt Citrine's eyes burn into the side of my face. I completely understood that the nature of this assignment required our absolute focus. I plucked a photo of a building that harkened back to the days of an Old-World bordello from the pile on the table. Citrine cleared her throat and sniffed as she held up a photo of a sailor in uniform.

"Tonight's assignment is no-kill. We're to find information on the trafficking ring: the who, what, why, and how. This person right here," she plucked down the photo of the sailor, "is Logistics Specialist Third Class Justin Lakewood. He's Navy but not much of a sailor, in the military sense. According to reports, however, he's one heck of a party planner/promoter." Citrine rolled her eyes as she spat out the words. "The parties he promotes house illicit dealings: drugs and sex with some weapons on the side, that sort of thing. You name it, he deals in it. It's amazing he has so much pull as an E-4."

"Honestly, it's not that far-fetched," Q responded, "most middle tier service members are the ears to the ground. They aren't quite 'leadership' but are 'leadership'. The younger tier looks at them as big time while the older establishment still regard them as youngins."

"He's an E-4, though," Citrine countered.

"Yeah, but E-4s are considered NCOs in the Navy while the rest of the branches don't," Quartz offered.

"Point goes to Q and I agree with his assessment. So, what does that make you, Staff Sergeant?" I teased as I picked up

Lakewood's profile and started to read. As I scanned his information, I gathered this dude was a box of rocks although he was very handsome. I could see how he could promote parties. So, that's how you do it.

"I'm on the cusp. Once I get promoted to E-6 status, I've officially crossed over to the dark side."

"As I was saying," Citrine interrupted, "this is the fish we have to catch. He's the key to a much larger network of fish. We must handle this delicately but expeditiously. We don't want to attract attention."

"So, what do you propose?" I took my eyes off the target's profile and leaned over.

"Q is our inside guy. He scored invitations to tonight's soiree, which is located at that building," Citrine pointed to the picture I just held in my hands. "We are to simply find Petty Officer Lakewood and find out what his role is within the ring. Nothing too major." She shrugged as if this was supposed to be this easy, but we all knew it was easier said than done.

I snorted and sucked my teeth. "Who's playing good cop and who's playing bad cop?"

"I'll let you decide since I ended your date too early."

"Cool. I'll play bad cop. What's Quartz's move?"

"He'll go ahead of us and scout the scene. His job is to blend in and gather more information about this ring. He'll let us know where the target's located."

Q stroked his chin and shook his head. "Copy all. Did y'all need anything else? I'll go ahead and check-in since the party is probably already in full swing. But I'll warn y'all now: there's a mixture of service members and civilians from babies to boomers so be prepared and act like you've seen it all before."

"Thanks, junior, but I think we can handle it. Any weapons allowed?" I rolled my eyes. He was like my little brother.

Q made a face at me while Citrine signaled dismissal to him. He jokingly gave me a salute and left. Once he cleared the area, Myrtle came back and escorted Citrine and me to another room full of sewing machines, bolts of cloth, and other sewing items. She moved aside a wall panel and unlocked a door, behind which was every type of weapon imaginable. I decided to take a necklace that doubled as a choking cord while Citrine chose a slim dagger.

"You ready for this?" Citrine hid the dagger in plain sight in her ponytail. She made the dagger look simultaneously alluring and functional as a hair pick. I clipped my necklace, so the pendant piece rested between my cleavage. "Let's go get 'em," I responded as I took one last look in the mirror. I grabbed the sneaker box and followed Citrine to the front of the store. We passed the counter on the way out and Citrine stopped me.

"Leave the box here; we can pick them up later."

An associate walked next to me and offered to grab the box from me. I gave her the box, and she disappeared to the back of the store.

When we walked out of the store, Citrine looked up the address for the party and started to walk. She put her phone in her purse. "Feel better?"

"Indeed!" My feet were singing the praises of these shoes.

"I can tell. You're no longer hobbling like a toddler wearing their mama's shoes." She chuckled as I stuck my tongue out and rolled my eyes.

"Look, it was my first time wearing those heels and I had a date, which you interrupted. Besides, they were coming off after a couple of hours anyway."

"Perhaps. Maybe your date would want to fuck you with those stilettos on." I did a double take when my brain registered what she said. I must have made a funny face because Citrine howled. She waved me off.

"Either way, I hope you were prepared for the evening. We both know how you get when you're around the opposite sex."

"Of course I was! Always prepared for any situation. Can't believe you think I wasn't."

"Girl, I was just playing."

As we bantered back and forth, the hairs on my neck suddenly stood at attention. I felt we were being watched. Citrine's face matched my spirit. An old lady seated behind a table in one of the alleyways summoned us. As if in a trance, we moved in unison toward her.

I studied her appearance as we got closer. She looked otherworldly, as if she was trying to find her identity in the modern world. I stared into her pale eyes and saw a thousand lifetimes. She gestured to two chairs in front of her. Intrigued, I sat down and Citrine followed. She stared into my eyes; her voice sounded like a roar from a waterfall.

"Why did you stop writing?"

Her stare unnerved me as I opened my mouth to answer. The words refused to come out. I was bewildered but couldn't answer the question because I didn't know the answer. I was taken aback as she placed her hands palms up on the table. How did she know I used to write? I never published anything. I lowered my hands into hers as she kept eye contact.

"Never throw away your gift; it will save you in the end."

With that, she turned over my hands and examined my palms. She let go of my left hand and inspected my right. She enclosed my right hand with both of hers and leaned forward.

"Beware of the thorns as you journey through the valley. Remember what you've learned, hang onto and trust your friends, and you will be victorious. Abandon them and it will cost you everything."

I sat back in awe because I understood what she meant. I froze in the chair as the lady sat back in hers and looked at Citrine. She held out her hands, and Citrine placed hers on top. The woman dropped the right and studied the left. While she examined her hand, she hummed softly.

She turned it over, abruptly stopped humming, and stared into Citrine's eyes.

"Don't stray from the chosen path. The day you do, you'll never return."

The woman leaned back in her chair and closed her eyes. As we stood and walked away, neither of us spoke. Whatever that was—it followed us.

CHAPTER 7

La Dama Roja/La Puerta Obscura

Citrine and I arrived at the address, both of us hesitating as we took in the building. It looked abandoned—windows dark, paint faded, a wrought iron balcony that had surrendered to rust. But there was something in the bones of it, something too deliberate in its disrepair.

Spanish details clung to the facade like stubborn ghosts: carved columns, cracked mosaic tiles, an archway that might've once welcomed men into a bordello or sanctuary. The line between the two felt thin here. We exchanged a look.

"Careful. Anomaly detected," Crystal's voice filtered through my earpiece, low and clipped. "You're being watched."

I didn't turn immediately. I let the feeling settle. Heavy, expectant. Then, slowly, I pivoted.

Across the street, a man slumped against a pole. His coat was two sizes too big and at least a decade too old. Eyes sharp beneath the grime. A smile broke across his face—something feral and knowing. Yellow teeth flashed like currency.

"Ladies," he rasped, "you're at the right place." He cackled. "Yessss… y'all are gonna have a good time."

Citrine crouched and handed him a folded bill. A smooth motion, practiced. The man accepted it with a raspy cough, tucking the money into a coat pocket like it wasn't the first time he'd been tipped for being creepy.

"Thank you kindly," he muttered. The street fell quiet again as Citrine gave me a slight nod. We stepped up to the heavy red door, where a towering manservant in a black suit waited like a wall.

"Ladies," he said, his voice smooth but guarded. "What brings you here?"

Citrine opened her purse and handed over the invitation. He scanned it with a small handheld device. A soft beep, a green light, and then—his grin.

"Welcome to La Dama Roja. Enjoy." He motioned toward the elevator and pressed the button for us.

"Have fun," he said as the doors slid shut behind us.

The elevator whisked us upward in silence. Velvet-lined walls. Gold fixtures. Everything designed to seduce. When the doors opened, another host stood waiting, impeccably dressed, eyes sharp.

"Buenas noches," he greeted us with a slight bow. From his pocket, he produced two playing cards. He handed one to me: Seven of Hearts. Citrine received a Five of Clubs.

"Be advised," he said, voice light but firm. "You must keep your card on you at all times. No transfers. No exceptions."

I turned the card between my fingers. "What's it for?"

He smiled. "Your ticket to the fun." With that, he unhooked the velvet rope and stepped aside. "Enjoy, ladies."

We passed through a second red door—this one darker, heavier, the kind that didn't open unless it wanted to. We stepped into what could only be described as a trap.

Dimmed lighting pulsed in warm reds and gold, casting everything in a haze. Sweet, floral scents permeated the air as if trying to cover up something.

Around the room, guests reclined on velvet lounges, laughing, sipping jewel-colored cocktails, plucking candies and hors d'oeuvres from crystal dishes. Gold pig statues balanced trays of edibles. Snail patterns adorned the servers' silk robes. Goats frolicked across carved wall panels. Porcelain toads crouched under mirrored tables. Snake designs coiled along the drapes, emerald and ruby eyes catching the light. A tall painting of a lion chasing a gazelle hung proudly. Overhead, a grand peacock sculpture spread its tail like a golden halo, watching us all.

It felt like a damn nursery room but deranged.

Crystal's voice came through the earbud. "Commander, keep in mind the animal motifs. These animals are the animals that are used to symbolize the seven deadly sins."

I kept my face neutral as I noticed Citrine's steps slowing. I could feel the allure of the room pulling her in – her eyes were glassy and she was speechless. I laid a hand on her arm. a silent tether pulling her back to me.

From one of the corners, a host approached with suave voice that could make panties drop.

"Everything here is curated for your pleasure. No judgments, no consequences. Only indulgence."

I smiled, polite. "Very generous. We'll savor the view for now."

The host gave a knowing nod, not offended at all, and slid away to tend to easier prey.

Up above, I caught shadows behind mirrored glass. Hidden observers, watching us. We didn't stay long.

As we stepped through the exit, Crystal chimed one more time—low, almost proud. "Commander, you resisted. They noticed."

We entered the next room. The dance floor was massive. Bodies pressed together in rhythm, sweat and perfume tangling in the air as the DJ spun the latest hits. The bass pulsed through the floor and surged up my spine. The beat wasn't just heard— it lived and breathed. For a second, I felt light. Like I was being absorbed by the crowd, about to lose myself in the moment.

Crystal's voice snapped me back. "Commander, remember why you're here. Observe. Do not participate."

I blinked hard, refocusing. Across the crowd, I spotted Citrine. She gave me a thumbs up but even from here, I could see the heat rising off her skin. She was fanning herself with her hand. I pushed through and leaned into her ear.

"Keep your head on a swivel."

She nodded. Then I felt a tap on my shoulder. Quartz. Cool as ever, blending in like he was born for this. To sell the cover, I pulled him in for a hug and kissed his cheek.

"Glad to see you made it."

He didn't waste time. "See the exits?" He nodded toward one of the glowing red signs. "There are seven of them."

I scanned the perimeter. He was right. Seven exits, each spaced evenly around the dance floor.

"Yeah!" I yelled over the music. Damn, this beat was addictive.

"They lead to seven distinct hallways. That's where you'll get the real info. But be careful—nothing's what it seems." Then he vanished into the crowd.

"Crystal," I murmured, "what's behind those exits?"

"According to building schematics: seven corridors. Once inside, they interconnect. If you and Citrine enter through one, you can loop through all the rooms without going back through the floor."

Perfect.

I grabbed Citrine's hand. "Heard there are quieter rooms in the back. Let's check them out."

She nodded, and we wove through the crowd toward the center exit. I tried the handle. Locked.

I frowned and tried again, pushing harder. No luck.

Citrine snapped her fingers like she'd solved a riddle. She pulled her playing card from her dress and held it over the door handle.

Click. The lock disengaged.

"Access granted," she smirked.

As the door clicked shut behind us, the music from the dance floor softened to a dull thump, like a distant heartbeat. The hallway ahead was dimly lit, but I could already see where the light shifted from one hue to the next—seven colors bleeding softly into one another along the corridor.

I pressed my hand to the wall to steady myself. The sudden quiet made the lightheadedness worse, not better. Everything felt slow. Velvet. Almost dreamlike.

Citrine caught me by the elbow.

"Hey. You okay?"

My voice came out thinner than I wanted. "Yeah. Just... that floor was intense."

"You're flushed. Adrenaline or... something else?"

Crystal's voice chimed in like a thread of steel. "Commander, your heart rate spiked. You've likely been exposed to a mild contact agent. Nothing lethal, but you're compromised. Stay close to Citrine."

I leaned against the wall and took a breath. "We stick together," I said. "Girls like us don't come alone anyway. We'd raise suspicion."

Citrine smiled, but it didn't reach her eyes. "We blend, we move, we observe. Just like training."

Together, we stepped into the corridor of sins.

CHAPTER 8

Corridor of Sins

I nodded as an orange glow from one of the rooms summoned me to explore. I pulled Citrine with me as I opened the door.

Inside was a feast dripping in decadence and glamor. Paintings of pigs lined the walls. Golden pig statues stood guard over glistening dishes. The orange velvet furniture begged us to sit, indulge, stay for a while. I'd already eaten—but in this room, that didn't matter. I could always eat a little more. It felt harmless. Expected, even. After all, what kind of host doesn't feed their guests?

Citrine elbowed me and whispered, "I think this is the desserts room. I bet all the rooms are themed around food." Her eyes lit up as she dragged me toward a particular table. She picked up a perfect praline, eyes wide with nostalgia.

"Pralines! I haven't had these in forever!" Before I could respond, her teeth sank into it. Her eyes rolled back in delight. "Oh. My. God. This is it."

As she melted into the praline, I spotted an apple jelly cake—and something in me stopped. A memory rose: my grandmother in her kitchen, spreading apple jelly over a hot cake instead of frosting—frosting was a luxury, jelly melted easier. She always ate it with strong, sugared coffee, no cream.

I cut a slice and grabbed a fork. Out of nowhere, a server appeared beside me, dressed in crisp white and black with a gold pig-head pin on his lapel.

"Coffee, madam?" he asked smoothly.

Red flag. "How did you know?" I asked, narrowing my eyes.

He smiled.

"We anticipate our guests' wishes. Besides, that cake is a Tidewater thing. Only people from there eat it. Others see it as poor man's food."

I said nothing. I didn't want to dishonor my grandmother— or risk her haunting me for disrespecting her signature dish. I took the cup.

The coffee was smooth, warm, and familiar. Paired perfectly. One bite became another. And another. Each sip made me feel cozy. Home. Safe. Too safe.

As I reached for another slice, Crystal's voice sliced through the haze in my ear. "Commander, there are other rooms to explore. I need a full scan to complete my analysis."

I froze. "You're right," I murmured, setting the fork down. I scanned the room. Citrine had migrated to the bananas foster station, licking her fingers. I approached her. "Girl, let's explore these other hallways. If this one's this good, imagine the rest."

Her mouth was full, but she managed to nod and swallow. "You're right. Wonder what the next hallway is?" She dropped her fork on the plate and linked her arm through mine.

✳✳✳

"This way." I jerked my head.

We passed by several others, each one dedicated to a specific indulgence: red meat, chicken, pork, seafood—even a vegetarian spread. I caught glimpses of guests lost in gluttonous bliss, their eyes glazed over, their mouths full. As we hurried past, the hallway beyond them shimmered with smoke.

"Let's see where this goes," Citrine whispered, clutching my hand tighter.

"Girl, it'll be alright." I released her grip, shook the tension from my fingers, and grabbed her hand again—firmer, grounding us both.

A lavender haze wrapped around us like a spell. The air was thick, fragrant with layers of scent: tobacco, cherry, grape, chocolate, vanilla—something else, deeper and ancient.

Crystal crackled into my ear, as steady as always.

"The scent profile includes cigar tobacco, vanilla, cloves, orange, myrrh, frankincense, assorted hookah blends… and opium. The room with the caterpillar over the door is the opium den. Avoid it. The safest route is the jazz lounge marked with a snail. Cigar smoke only."

Of course Citrine had her eye on the poetry slam. I steered her right—away from that seductive danger—and towards the snail.

We stepped into a world of blue haze and silver shadows.

A woman in a lavender slip dress stood on stage, her hair swept to the side, adorned with a cascade of blue poppies. The flowers trailed down like silk ribbons, delicate and dreamy. Behind her, a live quintet played—saxophone, upright bass, keys, soft snare. It was music that made you exhale.

Her voice was molten velvet, laced with sorrow. She sang of love lost and time wasted, of still nights and slow ruin. Each note pulled on some part of me I'd thought long buried.

We found a table tucked in the corner and sat down. The space was dressed in pale gray and misty blues, with thick curtains, art deco furniture, and golden snail motifs peeking from the shadows. It felt like a speakeasy for the soul-tired, a place where the world could forget you.

I scanned the room. No immediate threat, just temptation in velvet and smoke.

Citrine, however, was gone. Not physically—but emotionally adrift. Her eyes locked on the stage, lips parted slightly in awe.

I didn't blame her.

Even I felt my thoughts drifting. Drifting toward Silverback—my first love, my first betrayal. The man who gave me the world, then tried to take it from me piece by piece. He was gone. Dead by my hand. And still, there were nights I missed him.

A waiter approached, silent and smooth, placing two glasses on our table. The drinks shimmered blue, almost glowing.

He wore a snail lapel pin.

Citrine raised a brow. "We didn't order these."

"Complimentary," he said with a low smile. "Everyone who visits the jazz lounge receives a Blue Poppy. Enjoy." He vanished before we could object.

Citrine eyed the drink suspiciously, then looked at me. "What do you think?"

Crystal answered before I could.

"It's safe—for now. They don't drug the first one. But this should be your only one."

I picked up my glass and tilted it toward the light. The surface rippled like silk. "Let's just sip," I said. "If anything feels off, we stop."

Citrine clinked her glass gently against mine. "To velvet traps."

I smiled faintly. "And silent exits."

We sipped—and let the music carry us for just a moment more.

The band took a break, the last smoky note of the saxophone trailing off into the haze. Conversations resumed, low and buzzing like wasps. Citrine leaned in toward me, voice barely audible over the lull.

"Wanna see what's down the gold hallway?"

I gave a nod. "Let's get it."

We slipped out of the lounge and into the corridor lined in decadent gold. The walls shimmered as if dusted with crushed coins. Gilded toad statues crouched in the corners, smug little sentinels with ruby eyes and open mouths as if waiting for an offering.

As we stepped deeper in, the air changed. Thicker. Electric. Inside, it was like stepping into a private casino tucked in a fever dream.

Poker tables to the left, velvet green with flicking chips and low muttered bluffs. A roulette wheel spun in the back, clacking like bones on bone. Blackjack dealers, all sharp tuxedos and colder eyes. A spades game to the right was getting rowdy—cackling, slapping cards, accusations of reneging tossed around like confetti.

"Look at this place," Citrine whispered. Her eyes gleamed almost as much as the room.

Even the floor was a mosaic of gold coins—some real, some illusions. We walked carefully, like one wrong step might cost us more than just balance. Above us, a chandelier shaped like a toad's open mouth held hundreds of dangling poker chips, swaying slightly as if the room itself were breathing.

A dealer at the blackjack table caught my eye. She tapped the table with one long, lacquered nail. "You play?"

I gave her a smile. "Not tonight."

"Suit yourself, Jemeka," she purred.

I froze. Citrine's head snapped toward me.

That name hadn't been used since…

The dealer winked. "Word travels fast in a room like this."

I gave a short nod and pulled Citrine along. We didn't have time for games, literally or figuratively.

But the deeper we walked in, the harder it was to ignore the room's pull. Desire wrapped in possibility. Every laugh, every gasp at a flipped card, every clink of a chip said, *You could win. You could take it all.*

Only thing was… *what would it cost?*

We decided to enter a room with the biggest toad statue I'd ever seen. A fat toad perched on a lily pad, gold and smug, keeping a watchful eye over the crowd like it owned the place.

This was the poker room. A sea of velvet-covered tables stretched out before us. Waiters glided by with crystal glasses and silver trays, delivering everything from cigars to champagne. The dealers looked impeccable, their black velvet vests over crisp golden shirts, expressions unreadable.

I hovered by one of the tables, watching a hand unfold. Chips clicked, cards flipped. It was hypnotic.

Until Citrine elbowed me. She nodded toward the far end of the room.

That's when I saw it. A golden door. Standing in front of it was a man in a tailored suit and a toad lapel pin. Stocky, wide-set eyes, permanent smirk—he *looked* like a toad.

"Let's see what's in there," Citrine said.

We approached. He held up a hand. "Do you have your card?"

We flashed our cards. He scanned them, then stepped aside.

The room beyond was quieter. Cooler. More refined, but more dangerous. Shadows clung to the corners. Crystal's voice sliced through the haze.

"This is the high-stakes table. Each Greed room has one. From what I gathered, this is where the real information is."

A host gestured us toward a viewing gallery. We had a full view of the main table, a sleek black oval lit from above.

Damn, this setup was *sexy*.

I could feel tension heavy in the air like perfume. No one talked. Every card placement was deliberate, almost theatrical. I wasn't even playing, but the rush? Real.

I caught myself wishing I was here with Paul instead. As that thought passed, a scuffle snapped me back.

The dealer raised a hand. Security swarmed.

"Notice that?" Crystal's voice was hushed. "No guards visible, but they came quick. Look around casually."

I did. Citrine nudged me hard.

"Ow."

"Statues," she whispered. "The eyes are shifting. Red lights too. Surveillance."

"The lapel pins," I added. "They're glinting."

The dealer spoke, voice calm but cutting. "Gentlemen, we don't do that here. If you wish, you may settle your disputes in the *red hallway*."

One man scoffed, tossed his jacket, and stormed off. The other stayed, mumbling as his date rubbed his shoulder. She looked way too young to be with him.

The first man reappeared, pointed at them. "I'll see you before the night's over." Then he was gone.

Citrine leaned over. "Yo, is there a bathroom?"

I blinked. "Honestly… I need it too."

We flagged a waiter. He gave us directions and reassured us, "Don't worry, your table will be saved."

The bathroom was just as lavish. Crimson and black clashed like rival queens, both trying to dominate. My ancestors whispered again. My spirit was unsettled.

As we washed our hands, two older women emerged from the stalls, mid-conversation.

"This evening is starting off quite well," one said. "Have you seen the lot?"

The other giggled. "Oh yes. Some beautiful gems in the auction tonight. Usually, I wouldn't get a chance to snag these at work, but tonight? No rules."

They laughed, deep and full. Citrine and I exchanged a look.

Then the women turned toward us.

"You two looking forward to the auction?"

"Yes, of course," Citrine said, smooth as butter. "It's our first time."

"Oooh!" the first woman squealed. The second clapped. "Then you're in for a treat. Just keep an open mind, darling."

Their smiles were too wide. The kind that hid teeth.

They waved goodbye and disappeared into an emerald hallway.

Citrine cocked her head. "What do they mean by gems? Wanna go find out?"

I shook my head. "Naw, that's too obvious. They said that for a reason. Let's not spring the trap just yet."

"What makes you think it's a trap?"

"C'mon. How many women, especially upper echelon women do you know act like that?" Citrine scrunched her face as I continued.

"Those are military women. No imagination with the dresses they wore. Sensible shoes, and they looked worn. Did you see the haircuts?"

Citrine face went from confused to enlightened. "I see it now! The auction is the trafficking. But how do we know who's on the lot? How do they bid?"

I shrugged. "The only way to find out is to explore more rooms." I stopped myself. Should we compare notes just yet? I know I needed to take a beat before we explore any more hallways.

Citrine looked at me. "You know, something doesn't feel right. But each room is distinct. There were moments I was worried I couldn't pull myself out. You had to save me a couple of times. Maybe—"

I grabbed her shoulders. "Stop it. Now. You're human and it happens. I got pulled in a couple of times. It doesn't mean you aren't doing a good job. I need you to focus."

She took a couple of deep breaths. "You're right. I'm just being stupid. What do we know?"

"The rooms are based on the seven sins, each with the color and animal associated. Gold and toads? Orange and pigs? Grey and snails and caterpillars? The atmosphere, the room assignments, all point to them."

"Interesting. If I remember correctly, pigs represent gluttony. Toads represent greed. So what was the jazz and snails? I liked that room."

"Sloth. It was slow and the smells. Remember the caterpillar in Alice in Wonderland?"

Citrine snapped her fingers. "Of course! That makes sense. I'm guessing when the dealer told them to go to the red hallway, that's the anger."

"Good point. Should we go to the red room?"

Citrine tapped her cheek. "Instead of the green or red hallway, maybe the deep blue hallway. That one may be lust. The anger, envy, and pride hallways may be too intense."

I knew what she was getting at and I agreed. "Yeah. Let's check out the deep blue sea." I linked arms with her and she steered me down the blue hallway.

The hallway, bathed in sapphire blue, invited us to explore. The neon sign above read *Temptation Avenue*. Each room catered to some sort of fetish: touch room, scent room, whisper room, music room, sight room, and full immersion.

Temptation Avenue lived up to its name. I wanted to explore all the rooms. My body yearned to explore each forbidden pleasure, but my mind snapped back to reality. This wasn't the time or place to entertain desire. The last time I did, my lover was shot in the head.

We sped down Temptation Avenue, trying not to get pulled into another room. Then, a voice, low and familiar, cut through the noise.

"Jemeka. Come explore me."

I froze.

That voice! Too familiar, a little lighter than Silverback's but still with the suaveness that attracted me to him. It slid down my spine like warm silk and lust slammed into me like a wave as I remembered his lips—full, succulent, deliberate. Without thinking, I released Citrine's hand and drifted into the room.

The space was dimly lit, drenched in soft purple and flickering gold. The scent of sandalwood and vanilla hung in the air, wrapping around me like heat. Drapes of burgundy, violet, and navy floated from the ceiling. A painting of Pan dancing with nymphs stretched across the far wall, alive with movement, inviting indulgence.

At the center of the room stood a curved wooden chair. I ran my fingers across its back and a strange warmth stirred inside me.

Then, the voice again, silk-wrapped steel.

"I knew you couldn't resist."

I turned. From the shadows, a masked man emerged—his shirt was unbuttoned, sleeves rolled up like he had work to do. His chest was broad and bare, dusted with just enough hair to keep your eyes there too long.

My breath caught. He stepped closer. Every inch of my control fought to stay upright.

"Do you trust me?" he asked, voice low, hypnotic.

Crystal screamed in my ear: *"Hell no."*

But my head nodded anyway.

He took my hand and guided me gently to the chair. I sat, heat rolling under my skin.

He placed his fingers on my forehead.

"Relax."

I exhaled as he slid a satin blindfold over my eyes. The fabric caressed my skin, warm and soft.

"Nothing will happen unless you want it to, Angel."

His voice curled around me like incense. Then came the ropes—velvet this time—tightening gently around my wrists and thighs. Secure. Indulgent. Wrong.

Then—his hand slid up my throat and he kissed me. Hard. Deep. The kind of kiss that pulls secrets from your marrow.

He finished with a slow bite to my bottom lip.

"I see that call earlier didn't take long," he murmured.

I gasped. "I… I had to go over the details. I'm meeting them tomorrow."

He hummed, amused. "So you have all night?"

His hands explored my body, sparking every nerve. I writhed in the chair, wanting to reach back, touch him, *anchor* myself.

"This is only the beginning," he whispered.

Then, suddenly, my hands were free.

I ripped off the blindfold.

He was gone.

Confused, I stood, breathless. My fingers went to my chest—my card. Still there.

But something didn't sit right.

I stumbled into the hallway, heart racing, head buzzing. The guilt burned hotter than the kiss. Crap! Where the hell was Citrine?

Just as I turned to search for her, Citrine stumbled out of one of the rooms, dazed. Her eyes were glassy, and something in them betrayed more than she wanted to say.

"Damn," she muttered. "I'm sorry I let go of your hand. I saw someone I used to know." Her voice cracked slightly. "She's a stripper now. Used to be in my troop. Good kid. I always wondered what happened to her."

She paused, like the story needed room to breathe.

"Turns out, this is her side hustle. She's got a kid now. Military checks ain't stretching the way they used to. A lot of these girls… they're here for fast cash. Same story, different faces."

A tear welled and she wiped it away quickly, almost embarrassed.

I reached for her shoulder, grounding her. "And that's exactly the kind of information we need. This place recruits the vulnerable—the ones without a voice."

Just then, a server glided past, escorting a young woman and a man toward another hall. The rooms behind them glowed violet, soft and strange.

Citrine tilted her chin in their direction. "Wonder where they're going?"

I smirked, trying to pull her out of the heaviness. "Only one way to find out."

We linked arms, exhaled, and followed them into the next corridor.

***

The next corridor, as it turns out, wasn't the one with violet light. Instead, we were bathed in violent red. Not romantic red. Not lipstick, roses, or neon signs. War red. Deployment red.

The kind of red that flooded the ops center when everything was about to go to hell.

My gut clenched. So did Citrine's hand in mine.

Crystal's voice buzzed in my ear, calm but clipped. "Stay close to each other. It's dangerous here. Don't stop. Stay centered until you see green."

I squeezed Citrine's hand hard. Too hard. She winced but nodded like she understood.

We moved fast, resisting the pull to look left or right. But it was impossible to ignore the sounds: bones crunching, screams that came from the gut, not the throat. Animal sounds. Human rage.

One glance. That's all I allowed myself.

One room was a rage chamber—people breaking mirrors, bottles, furniture. Another had a boxing ring in the center, surrounded by spectators screaming for blood. No music. Just fists and fury.

The walls pulsed with red light, like a heartbeat on the edge of stroking out.

As I took mental notes, a bare-chested man stumbled into our path. His eyes were wild, blood streaming from his temple. He laughed, a deep, broken sound, and took a step toward us.

I shifted into fight stance, ready to drop him.

"Stay away from the walls. Stay centered." Crystal's voice rang in my ear again.

The man turned and slapped his palm against the wall.

Two black-gloved hands reached out from the shadows and yanked him into the wall.

He screamed once, high and panicked, before the wall slammed shut behind him like a steel trap.

Citrine's eyes went wide. She choked back a sound, clutching my arm now.

We kept moving.

The air was thicker now—musty, hot, choking. Lion roars echoed from unseen speakers, mixing with real growls and snapping teeth. Torn posters of lions littered the hallway. Gold-painted statues lay toppled and shattered across the floor.

The symbolism wasn't subtle.

Anger ruled here. Rage was god.

"Damn!" Citrine shouted over the chaos. "Will this hallway ever end?"

I didn't answer. I was wondering the same thing.

Then everything froze. The sounds cut out. The lights dimmed. The hallway held its breath.

Then came the chime.

Not the soft kind we'd heard before. This one was deep. Ominous. It vibrated in my ribs.

Crystal's voice returned—sharp, no time for calm.

"You have 30 seconds to get out. That's the final warning. All hell is about to break loose."

Shit.

I scanned ahead and finally saw it. A green door at the far end of the hall glowed faintly like a lifeboat.

"Quick! The green door!" I shouted.

We ran. When we reached the knob, it didn't budge. Locked.

Citrine fumbled for her card and waved it over the panel. A click. Best sound I'd heard all night.

"Once you go through the door," Crystal said, "do not look back."

We threw the door open, stepped through, and slammed it closed behind us just as the roar of chaos exploded again behind the walls.

Muffled screams echoed through the door.

Citrine and I looked at each other, breathing hard, hearts racing.

That… was too close.

***

After we reassessed ourselves, Citrine and I had to take a breather. That was much too intense. Luckily, the cool color of sea green foam calmed me down.

I felt a sharp pain in my side as Citrine nudged me again. Seriously, she needed to take a beat with that elbow. "This isn't like the other rooms. They had a hallway leading to the rooms; this one is a gigantic ball room."

I scanned the room and agreed. Crystal chandeliers, wallpaper with different shades of green. Slithering snakes twisted around glass cases that housed jewelry and other objects. The servers in this room wore snake bangles, necklaces, anklets, and bracelets wrapped around a body part.

Citrine held onto my hand tight. "Unlike other rooms that dealt with shadows and smoke, this room here is on full display in clear view."

She was right. No overwhelming scents. No smoke. Nothing to hide.

"Let's stay focused," I whispered, "clearly, something here requires innate attention."

Citrine loosened her grip as we walked through the gallery, admiring the scenery. Suddenly, I stopped in my tracks. I blinked twice, making sure I saw what I saw.

"What? What is it?" Citrine murmured.

I was mortified as I studied the case. The case seems to be made from ice. On further inspection, the card imprisoned in that case was my card. To add to the horror, a snake seductively slithered around the case as if protecting it. His tongue flicked at me as if it read my mind, wondering if it was real.

I didn't lose the card. I had it on me the entire time per the host's instructions. No replacements and no transfers. Unless…while I enjoyed the pleasures of the Whisper Room, Paul switched them somehow.

Crystal confirmed my thoughts. "Yes, you've been compromised. While the number and suit are the same, the card is not. The original was made of thicker cardstock, to embed the encoder undetected. The one in your possession is made from thinner paper. It feels the same but turn it lengthwise."

I did as instructed and she was right. It was different.

As I mulled over the mystery, I overheard two men deep in conversation.

"This auction is going splendidly."

"Oh, I definitely agree. I had a chance to look over the lots and I found Lot 7H most intriguing."

"Bold choice considering it's brand new. Hopefully, you left enough for the rest of us." They shared a lighthearted chuckle as they moved on.

Crystal jumped in as I made mental notes of the conversation. "Observe the description below each display."

I skimmed the description and realized this was not an object. It was a 20-year-old woman. I pulled Citrine to another display and read the description. This one was for a young boy 22-25 years old.

I gasped.

Citrine narrowed her eyes and then her face darkened. "These aren't objects they are selling. They're people. This is way more than I could have imagined."

Before I could open my mouth, a chime sounded. Or, chime wasn't the right word – it was more like a gong. All stopped in their activities and listened.

"Attention patrons. The following lots have been purchased: 7H, 5C, 9S, 3D, and AC. There is still time to place bids on the other lots. Spend wisely. Thank you for your patronage."

Citrine and I looked at each other. After reading the descriptions, we were supposedly bought.

"Citrine, the lot numbers correspond with our cards. I have the seven of hearts, which equals 7H. You have five of clubs…5C. And those descriptions are us!"

My blood ran cold as Citrine grabbed her ponytail and started to smooth it. "I think we need to leave. This is getting dangerous for us."

I contemplated her suggestion but we had to get all the information about this place. "Look, this is the last room. Let's see where it goes."

"But we'll be separated. How can we help each other if one of us is in trouble? And have you seen that couple we were trying to follow? What happened to them?" Her voice went up an octave.

Crystal entered the chat via my ear. "Commander, she's nervous. She has a point, but the benefits outweigh the risks. According to their database, no one has expired. Recommend keeping eyes open and mouth shut until the end of the night."

Both made excellent points. Citrine had every right to be nervous. We'd both been through things our training didn't prepare us for. I didn't consider that scenario because neither one of us knew what's behind the doors. But Crystal was able to go places Citrine could not. And if Crystal said the benefits outweighed the risks, we should complete the mission.

A tap on my shoulder interrupted my thoughts. I casually looked over my shoulder and saw a young man dressed in a designer suit easily worth at least $5000, including shoes and jewelry. He flashed a smile, but his eyes remained sinister.

"Madam. Your presence is requested in the Peacock room to meet your patron. If you would please follow me." He gestured. I looked at Citrine. Her eyes said *don't go and don't leave me* but her posture had all the confidence in my abilities.

I smiled back at her and squeezed her hand, letting her know we were going to be ok, then followed the gentleman out the room. We walked down a hallway in silence. We stopped in front of a gold door, emblazoned with a peacock. He punched in a code and it opened to another room. The next door resembled a gilded cage. He fished a key out of his pocket and unlocked it. We walked past a few doors before he pointed me to my assigned room, decorated with plumage on the front door.

I thanked him as I entered. The lights flickered on, indicating the room was motion sensored. The soft lighting reoriented my senses as my gaze drank in my surroundings.

The room was perfectly curated. Sumptuous furniture, decked in teal, emerald, and grape. The lamps were adorned in jewels. A golden writer's desk equipped with gold plated notebooks, peacock feathers as quills, and different hues of ink sat in the corner, inviting to sit down and write. The writer in me almost obliged, especially when I spied a vintage record player with loads of records ranging from jazz to old school R&B. Nothing would complete me more than to sit down and write while A Night In Tunisia plays in the background.

Crystal grounded me at that moment. "Remember, nothing is as it seems. Proceed with caution, Commander."

I nodded as I resisted the urge. I turned my attention to the walls. Paintings of peacock, goats, and nymphs were prominently displayed. But something was off with the next picture. On closer inspection, it was me, Silverback, and a mutual friend. I took a step back and saw multiple pictures of me and Silverback, me and the mutual friend, and just me. My numerous promotion letters, awards, and decorations were splayed all over the wall. I caught my breath as I studied the picture of me and Silverback, my former abuser and lover. He was shot dead by my best friend and betrayer after we made love.

Confused, I wondered why this room was about me. I tried to remember the name of the mutual friend but it was such a long time ago.

I was engrossed in trying to remember when I heard a deep southern voice.

"I'm surprised you didn't sit down at the desk and start writing."

I whirled around to find the mutual friend. Hair cut in a Caesar with deep waves, the timbre of his voice sounding like God himself. His suit...chef's kiss. From the Marc Jacobs collection. He smelled of chocolate strawberries and roses. His name came to me in a rush.

"Marcel!" I froze. Marcel Chardonnay was a mutual friend of Silverback's. As much as I wanted to test drive, I couldn't do it, especially after the debacle between Silverback and Wolf.

"Hey, gorgeous. Glad to see you're doing well." He sat down on one of the sofas and crossed his legs. His eyes smiled while his face remained stone.

"I haven't seen you in forever. Hold on," my mind came back to reality. "Did you just buy me?"

"Not you per se. Just your time. I know after James's death, you were affected. I reached out to you but you are so difficult to find. I had to use my contacts. They told me you relocated here as a consultant to a firm."

Consultant to a firm? I only used that cover with Paul. Somehow, he and Paul were connected.

"Well, I'm glad you found me. What's been new with you? Are you still in the Army?"

"Yeah, running big things but I'm retiring soon. Nothing too big."

We chatted but I can tell he was trying to get me at ease. Since we were at a stalemate, I decided to ask a question.

"So, why pictures of me? My stuff? Why the pictures on the wall?"

He laughed as if he was in on a secret. I raised my eyebrow. He cleared his throat.

"Something I realized about you a long time ago. There were times you weren't confident. After what James did to you, I was shocked you went back." He stood up and sat next to me. He grabbed my chin softly. "You're beautiful and deserved so much more. Even now, your eyes tell me you miss him, even after everything."

He leaned closer. "Women like you need to be reminded about how extraordinary you are. Which is why I having this room filled with your favorite things."

My face felt hot. Yes, he was a smooth talker. But I'd been through enough tonight that this conversation was child's play.

I crossed my ankles and tucked a loose strand of hair behind my ear. Marcel was just like Silverback — same hunger, same danger — but with more sugar. Silverback was forged in the streets of Baltimore. Marcel? He came up through the bayous of Louisiana. And just like sugar, Marcel melted in smooth…But too much of him? Might kill you.

I contemplated my next move but Marcel looked at his watch.

"Damn! Where did the time go?" He shifted his position and looked at me. "Our time is up. We can get out of here and talk more, or we can leave for the night. Totally up to you."

I sighed, thankful this night was coming to an end. "Let's call it a night. I'm about to fall asleep on you."

He snickered, which felt genuine. "Too much indulgence for one night?"

I cocked my head to the side as he offered an explanation.

"Paul works for me. It was his job to get you here after he found you."

My jaw hit the floor. "You watched us on our date?!" The fuck?

He leaned back with a smug grin. "Of course I did! I've watched you all evening."

I felt flattered and disgusted at the same time. I needed a shower…pronto. Yet something about this was magnetic and sexy.

I pulled myself together and leaned in. "How about this: now that you know where I am, why don't we set up a time outside of here?"

"That'll be amazing. You got Paul's info. Just talk to him." He stood up as if he was about to leave.

"But," I placed my hand on him, "it will mean much more to me if I hear your voice instead of a cold text from Paul."

I stood up and slithered over to the door.

"Wait. How do I do that?"

"Get it from Paul." I shrugged and left the room without giving him a chance to respond.

I found my way upstairs and left the elevator. As I reached for the exit, I waved goodbye to the bouncer.

"Did you have fun?" His smile gleamed.

I stretched my arms. "So much so I'm exhausted."

"I'm glad. Have a good night!"

I opened the door but quickly paused before turning around to face him. His brows raised in curiosity.

"Before I go, I got a question. Who and why La Dama Roja? What's the story? Especially when y'all just cater to exclusive clientele." I was a sucker for historical buildings and the stories behind them.

His face beamed as his chest swelled. "This building was owned by Amelia Reyes-Ramos. During colonial times, it used to be a restaurant/tavern on the top floor, which was open to the public. Red was her favorite color, so to distinguish her establishment from the rest, she painted the door red and always wore red. But down below were for the thieves, the dreamers, mavericks, heathens, outsiders. Amelia welcomed them all. A place where everyone was accepted, no matter the person's status. She also helped slaves run up North to freedom. She was a keeper of secrets, up until her last breath at 92. Her family still owns the building and carries on the tradition."

Wow. What a story. I plucked two hundred dollars from my bra and stuffed it in his breast pocket.

"Thank you." I don't think he has any idea the level of debauchery that's downstairs.

He tapped the pocket, kissed my hand, and bid me a good night.

As soon as I stepped into the night, the air enveloped me in cool breezes. Citrine leaned against a light pole, her face relaxed.

"Ponytail still in place." I hugged her, doing a quick body scan for both of us. Neither one was shaking.

"And we still look amazing!" Citrine followed.

We laughed but it was from shock. Shock we made it. Shock this stuff even happens. Shock we'd had front row seats.

"You know what we used to do back home?" Citrine linked her arm through mine.

"Oooh! Let me guess! An after-hours breakfast spot?"

"Girl! I almost forgot you from the south! What you say?"

"I could crush some ham and eggs with waffles right now."

Citrine grinned. "I know a spot that will cater to our needs! Who's driving, me or you?"

"Do you feel up to driving?" I felt the weight of the world in my bones, but I had to check on Citrine and make sure she was straight.

"How about we call a ride?" Then she lowered her tone. "We're still being watched. If we just partied, we may not want to drive."

That's why I loved me some Citrine. "Call in the cavalry and see if they can drive our cars back to our respective places."

"I'll leave my car here and spend the night with you since you're closer. Remember appearances."

Crystal answered. "Agree with Citrine's plan. More conspicuous. And she's right: you two are still being watched."

The plan made sense. I just hadn't had a sleepover for a while. I did welcome the company though.

"Fine. But you better not snore."

"You won't even know I'm there. Let me make a call." She pushed a few buttons on her phone. "Wipe your phone," she said quietly. I nodded and reset everything to factory default mode.

We stumbled down the sidewalk — mostly because Citrine had insisted on wearing heels all night.

A few minutes later, our ride pulled up. Chrys jumped out, opened the back door, and made sure we were in safely before circling to the driver's side.

"Took y'all long enough," she teased. "Looks like you had an interesting night." She glanced back at Citrine. "Oh, and your slippers are under the seat."

"You remembered?!" Citrine slipped off her heels and sighed in relief as her feet found the plush ballet flats.

I giggled. "Okay, there's a story here."

They told me about Citrine's wild night in Miami — club-hopping with her old handler, Jade. Refused to ditch the heels, danced five hours straight, and ended up with feet swollen like suckling piglets. Jade called Chrys, who was coincidentally in Miami. Not only did Chrys bring fluffy shoes, she also *rescued* them when some creep tried to grab Citrine outside the club.

"She whooped that ass," Citrine added proudly. "Then drove us straight to safety. Been my getaway girl ever since."

We rolled into a lowkey breakfast joint called The Morning Rooster. Family-owned, quiet, no flash. Just the kind of place that served peace by the plate.

The server pointed us to a private room. The dragon centerpiece, the calming colors, the warmth of the space — it all worked on me like medicine.

The food arrived quickly. I blinked. "How'd they know what we wanted?"

"I called ahead," Citrine said, already forking into her pancakes.

My plate held everything I didn't know I needed: eggs drowned in gravy, sugar ham, pecan waffle, hash browns with onions.

I ate like I hadn't eaten in years. Chrys just sipped her coffee, smirking like a mom watching her kids destroy a buffet.

The comfort of the food, the stillness of the space, unlocked a memory — my first military assignment in Hawaii. A woman from my unit took me under her wing. Taught me how to walk into a room like I belonged there. Took me out, taught me how to eat, laugh, live. That night, she ordered Spam fried in teriyaki with eggs and rice. I'd never tasted anything so good.

She was amazing.

As Citrine and I compared notes — about the rooms, the people, the patterns — Chrys listened, quiet but dialed in.

The night had taken pieces of us. But in this room, over waffles and war stories, we started putting ourselves back together.

****

The elevator opened to my floor with a soft chime and for the first time that night, I let my shoulders drop.

Citrine kicked off her slippers the second we walked in. "Remind me to burn those heels."

"Put it on the agenda right after 'save the world'."

The condo smelled like sage and sandalwood — my space, my silence. The city lights outside the window blinked against the glass like quiet applause.

Citrine flopped onto the couch, pulled out her burner phone, and tapped out a message.

Meeting tomorrow at 1000 hours. Complex. Be sharp.

"They've been warned," she said, stretching. "I'm crashing in the guest room. Good work tonight, partner."

I gave her a fist bump as I headed toward my bedroom. "You too. Proud of us."

She disappeared down the hall.

I slipped out of my clothes, pulled on an old tank top, and sat on the edge of my bed. The quiet felt earned.

"Crystal," I murmured.

"Yes, Commander?"

"Shut down for the night."

"All data collected tonight has been transmitted to your device at the Complex. A full dossier will be waiting in the morning."

I nodded, already halfway to sleep.

"You've done well, Commander. Rest easy."

"Good night, Crystal."

"Good night."

The room dimmed just a little more.

Mission complete. For now.

CHAPTER 9

Burn After Reading

I woke up the next morning to find that Citrine had already left. She left a note that she was picking up her car. I yawned and glanced at the wall clock. It read 0545. Great. This would've been a perfect day to sleep in — but we still had work to finish.

"Good morning, Crystal," I said as I stretched, pulling back the drapes to let the rising sun greet me.

"Good morning, Commander. Sleep well?"

I paused, thinking.

"Actually? Pretty good, considering."

"Yes, you two did have a wild night. Are you still meeting Citrine at 0800?"

"Let's move it to 0730. Gives us more time."

"Already sent. You should receive confirmation shortly."

Ding. The burner phone chirped.

"You read my mind. I'll grab breakfast."

"Awesome," I said. "Alright, Crystal. Time to get ready."

Showered, dressed, coffee in hand, I stepped out into the quiet morning. The streets still had that eerie 'after a storm' feel, but the street sweepers were already erasing the night's sins.

***

Citrine and I pulled into the Complex at the same time. After passing through security and boarding the elevator, she broke the silence.

"You feeling alright?"

"Surprisingly, yes. You?"

"Honestly? I feel like I let you down. I'm used to going after predators — abusers. This was different. I almost slipped more than once. Am I cut out for this?"

I turned to her, steady.

"Your feelings are valid. I felt the same way. That's why we lead — because we go through the fire and learn. We didn't fall in. We held our ground. And I wouldn't have done this with anyone but you."

She smiled softly.

"Thank you. I needed that."

The elevator doors opened.

"Let's pull everything together."

***

We entered Meeting Room 2. As promised, our phones were there, charged and ready.

Crystal chimed in. "I've uploaded the files to the server, Commander. Ready whenever you are."

I powered up my laptop and opened Crystal's folder. Every detail was organized, from notes and photographs to maps and schematics. Perfect.

I distributed taskings:

- The buyer list went to Lotus for deep background checks.

- The building schematics and surveillance went to Amethyst.

- Q handled compiling all digital footprints into a master report.

The team arrived like clockwork — Amethyst leading, Lotus behind. Q brought up the rear, flashing his thumb drive.

"Got everything compiled from last night," Q said.

"Perfect," I nodded. "Thank you all."

Lotus tilted her head.

"It's a small list — only ten buyers."

"Exclusive," Citrine added, furiously typing.

"Sounds about right for what we saw," I said as I synchronized everyone's inputs into a master file.

"A time was had," Q added dryly.

"No casualties reported," he added, glancing between us.

I sipped my coffee.

Damn. I've got a hell of a team.

Amethyst cleared her throat. "Ma'am, how would you like to structure the briefing? All-in-one? Individual briefings?"

"Everyone briefs their portion. Citrine will run the deck, I'll manage transitions. We'll build one product."

"Already created a secure folder," Amethyst added. "Labeled it *Assignment 1*. Private access."

"Excellent work," I said with a wink.

"What's the deadline for final inputs?" she asked.

"How long do you need?"

"Forty-five minutes," Q answered.

"Same here," Lotus added.

"Good. You'll have my complete deck in forty-five."

I smiled. "Appreciate you all."

Forty-five minutes later, the full product was ready. I pulled their files into the master deck and fine-tuned the flow:

- Amethyst: building layout & logistics

- Lotus: buyers & attendees

- Quartz: digital platform & auction system

- Citrine and I: field observations

I sent the final briefing order to the team for review. One by one, thumbs-up icons lit up on my screen.

With an hour to spare, I printed hard copies for everyone.

"Anyone need to run through notes before we step in?"

Confident head shakes.

Damn, this is why we win.

***

The door blew open as Sid led the way, followed by Pearl. I flipped the room status to *Occupied* and locked the door behind them.

Sid took the head seat with quiet authority. Pearl slid into the chair to her immediate right.

Sid leaned back and exhaled softly, pointing to the screen.

"Ready."

I stepped to the front, fist-bumping Citrine at the controls.

"Morning. This briefing covers the assignment we executed and our findings. My team will walk you through. Citrine and I will fill gaps as needed."

I sipped my water. Sid stayed perfectly still. Pearl allowed herself a small smile.

"Amethyst covers building logistics. Lotus will present on buyers. Quartz handles the digital systems. Citrine and I supplement field intel. If there are no preliminary questions, we'll begin."

I stepped aside as Amethyst took point.

Amethyst began. "La Dama Roja and La Puerta Obscura, mapped by sector. Controlled traffic flow. Zones include

Indulgence Parlor, Ballroom, Corridor of Sins, and the private Pride Rooms."

Slides clicked forward.

"Surveillance was extensive. Cameras at every junction. Entry and exit tightly controlled — including underground access."

Sid's brow twitched. Pearl sat motionless.

"Security acted more like handlers than staff. Military backgrounds probable."

Amethyst finished and sat. Lotus took over.

"Confirmed buyers: ten. High-net worth. Multiple foreign proxies, private security contractors, offshore accounts."

She displayed the profiles. "Two flagged for previous procurement suspicion. No formal charges filed."

Pearl tapped her index finger once on the tabletop.

Quartz followed. "Auction platform operates on an encrypted blockchain. Full anonymity. Funds routed through decentralized wallets into shell entities."

Code flashed behind him.

"More concerning — backend access taps into protected government data streams. Someone with serious clearance is feeding this network."

That's when Sid exchanged her first glance with Pearl. Subtle. Loaded.

Quartz sat.

I closed. "From the field, this operation was surgical. Not simply trafficking — targeted psychological acquisition."

I paused.

"The Corridor of Sins used personal vulnerabilities. Pride Rooms elevated select targets. Private histories were exploited."

I controlled my voice. "In my Pride Room, materials tied directly to my history with James were displayed."

Sid's eyes sharpened. She knew who James was. We all did.

"This wasn't random exploitation. This was targeted conditioning — asset grooming at scale."

The silence was absolute.

Pearl leaned back. "Understood."

Sid stood with her usual precision. "We'll escalate this to Glacier." Her gaze swept the room one final time. "This just went above our pay grade."

Without another word, Sid and Pearl exited.

We sat in the silence that followed. The soft hum of monitors filled the air.

I exhaled, scanning my team.

We survived the trap. But something much bigger was coming.

PART II

When Shadows and Games Collide

We don't survive the darkness by escaping it.
We learn its language.

PROLOGUE

Forget Me Not

It didn't matter what time of year I visited—Alaska's beauty always shone. I needed another reset, so Citrine and I booked a plane and flew into Anchorage. As soon as we stepped outside the airport, Citrine howled.

"Girl! What the fuck? It's freezing!"

I laughed as I kept walking. "We're up north! And it's only sixty-eight degrees." I pulled my suitcase behind me, scanning the lot for our rental.

"Girl, where I'm from, that's cold!" Citrine pretended to shiver dramatically.

We found the SUV, tossed our luggage in the trunk, and climbed in. Before I could start the engine, Citrine spoke again.

"Hey… I know how much visiting Emerald means to you. Just make sure you take care of yourself afterward." She blew into her hands for warmth.

My mind flashed back to when Emerald took me to my first Fur Rendezvous. The rides, the blanket tossing, the ice sculptures—everything unique about Alaska made me fall in love with this place. It made me smile, thinking of all the times I'd shared with my best friend.

"Winter was Emerald's favorite season. But I wanted to celebrate her during her favorite month."

Citrine took my hand in hers. "Then let's go celebrate her life under the midnight sun."

We drove to the military cemetery in silence. When we reached Emerald's gravesite, I shut off the engine and exhaled. Citrine patted my hand.

"Go on, Jemeka. She's waiting for you. I'll be here if you need me."

I nodded, grabbed the bouquet of flowers, and stepped out. I walked up to the headstone and placed the flowers down gently. My shoulders sagged as tears fell.

"I'm so sorry. I wish I'd been there when you needed me most. I wish I'd been the kind of friend you could come to for help." My mouth went dry.

A light touch lifted my chin. Through watery eyes, I saw my best friend. She shimmered faintly, as if made of soft light.

"Shhh," Emerald said, putting a finger to her lips. "There was nothing you could have done. I didn't come to you because you'd been through the exact same trauma. I didn't want to burden you."

She sat beside me as we stared at the headstone.

"I wanted to protect you from that part of my life. But in the end, this life found you anyway. And look how strong you've become. I'm so proud of you."

Her words were so comforting, I almost forgot she was gone. I cleared my throat. "It's so hard to go on without you. You taught me so many things."

Emerald tilted my face toward her. "I taught you to embrace who you are. Look at all the people you've helped. You're doing so well—this must be your calling. Don't stop. There are so many Jemekas and Emeralds out there who need you."

I wiped my eyes on my sleeve. "Will I ever see you again?"

Emerald stood and smiled. "I'm always here. Always watching. That's the beauty of being a spirit. All you have to do is talk." She glanced into the distance. "They're calling me. I've got to go."

She turned to leave but paused. "I love you, Jemeka. You were my best friend—and you always will be. Take care."

With that, she vanished.

A rush of relief poured over me. I stood and dusted myself off. Before heading back to the car, I looked up at the sky and mouthed, "Thank you."

When I reached the SUV, Citrine was already in the driver's seat. She jerked her head toward the passenger side. I climbed in and buckled up.

Citrine cruised out of the cemetery. We exchanged quiet smiles. No words were needed. Emerald was gone—but at least I still had Citrine by my side.

CHAPTER 1

All is Bright...For Now

Christmas was supposed to be a happy time. Lights glistening everywhere, fires burning, and the scent of woods and apples evoking memories of coziness and warmth. When there was snow, it only enhanced the magic of the season.

Gloominess reigned supreme, with bitter cold and wind. No smile or laughter protected you from the darkness within. I hated this time of year.

Don't get me wrong. I wanted to love this season. I wanted the happiness I saw across the faces. But, for some reason, it never worked out for me.

As I languished in my misery, my regular cellphone rang. I glanced at the caller ID and saw it was Citrine.

"What's good, my girl?" I tried to hide the joy in my voice.

"What's going on, baby?" That Creole New Orleans accent gets me every time.

"Just sitting here about to watch some TV and eat some ramen."

"Oh no, baby. Why you sitting at home alone? It's the holidays!"

"I know that! But I'm not feeling it this year."

"Something tells me you don't feel it any year."

I rolled my eyes. "Look. I never celebrated, and I just don't see the big deal."

"That's because you never experienced it. You may have been around it, but it never really touched you."

I paused as I reflected on that statement. She was right; I'd never experienced it. Suddenly, I heard a knock at the door.

Puzzled, I put down my phone and grabbed my gun. I wasn't expecting anyone and after what happened in Amsterdam, I'd been more cautious. I looked through the peephole and saw my girl looking back at me.

"Open the door, ma'am."

I put my gun away and opened the door. We hugged for a few minutes and I led her into my living room. After a few casual moments, the conversation took a serious turn.

"I came to check up on you. You went through a traumatic event and that's not an easy thing to get over."

"Well, no. It's not easy, but surprisingly, I'm numb to it."

Citrine crossed her legs underneath her as she rolled her eyes. "If that's what you're going to tell me, fine. But since you're on break and I'm on break… and Aster is on break and Peridot is on break…"

I raised an eyebrow. I'd partied with Citrine before, and it was a time. I'd never look at New Orleans the same again. I had always wanted to hang out with Aster and Peridot but schedules never seemed to align.

I smiled. "What did you have in mind? New Orleans again?"

Citrine laughed. "Naw! As much as I love my city, you've got to do Christmas in Europe! I got the tickets, the itinerary, everything. I just need you to come along!"

I had to admit her enthusiasm was contagious. I'd never been to Europe, and never had a bad time with Citrine. Before I could speak, Citrine got on her feet and grabbed my hand.

"Of course you're coming! Let's go!"

"I need to pack first! And I need to tell Pearl." I started to grab my phone as Citrine pulled me out of my apartment.

"Call her on the way. You know how travel works. Again, let's go!"

I put on some shoes and locked my door. When we got downstairs, I hopped in the car and Citrine ripped out of the parking garage. I had to hold on to the side handle as if we were a part of a Formula One race.

We got through security without any issues. We walked up to the Administrative building where I passed Ms. Magnolia. She smiled and nodded. I returned the gesture as Citrine and I got on the elevator. We went straight to a conference room and I saw Peridot, Moons, Sapphire, and Spin, her assistant. Morgan, from HR/Travel, was also there.

Sapphire stood in front, watching the clock. As soon as the big hand hit twelve, she turned and nodded to Spin. He shut the door and walked over to the computer. A PowerPoint briefing came alive on the screen. *Security briefing* it read.

"Welcome to your security brief. I'm Sapphire and I represent the Security Office. Please pay attention to the slides because they contain information needed for your trip. We need everyone back in one piece—not in pieces."

As she clicked through the slides, going over the dos and don'ts and the significant monuments in each country, I slowly realized these were all European countries: the United Kingdom, Belgium, and Germany. Hold on… were we going to the Christmas markets? Holy shit! I had always heard about the markets but never got a chance. Was that why we were doing a security briefing? I mean, we always did a security brief before we traveled. But three countries! Yes! I needed this.

"Onyx?" Sapphire's voice snapped me back to reality. Without a beat, I answered.

"Yes?"

"What are the official languages of Belgium?"

I sat back in my seat and smiled. "Dutch, French, and German. Depends on the region. Flemish is also used."

Sapphire raised her eyebrows and nodded. "Just checking." She smiled as she continued. So many things to remember: the etiquette, the security level, the customs. Sapphire wrapped up her briefing as Morgan from HR/Travel stepped to the podium with her iPad.

"Ladies, your tickets and itinerary have been forwarded to your respective devices. You will go in pairs. Please check your phone for your 'buddy assignments.' When you land, your concierge will meet you after you clear customs. Luggage will be waiting for you at your destination. Remember to bring a small carry-on with essentials. Any questions?"

Morgan scanned our faces. When we remained silent but giddy, she smiled and waved. "Have a great time and bring me back some chocolate!"

***

After we landed in London and cleared customs, I was shocked to see Wilhelm, our host from when I went to the Netherlands for my retreat.

"Wilhelm!"

"Whoa, now. That's Harry."

"Harry? I thought—"

Citrine cut me off. "He got promoted. His name is Harry now. As in Harry Winston. He's a jeweler. You know, taking care of the gems."

"Well, congrats! About damn time!" I laughed as I gave him a bear hug. He smelled amazing, like chocolate cherries.

We let go and I felt a tap on my shoulder. I whirled around and saw Aster. "Holy shit! You're here too?!" Another bear hug incoming.

"Oh yeah! Citrine told me about this trip and invited me. With the new assignment I got I wasn't too sure I would be able to go but lucky for me, Pearl let me have some down time and told me to 'scoot.' She ain't said nothing but a word!"

After a quick headcount, Harry clapped loudly. "Alright, ladies—there's someone else you should meet." He gestured behind him. A young man stepped forward, tall and trim, with a short Marine-style haircut. He wore a smart black peacoat over a neat travel uniform. His face was earnest, friendly, but a little wary. Like he was bracing for impact.

Harry threw an arm around him. "Everyone, this is Reed. Fresh out the Marines, where he was a culinary specialist. He's been learning the ropes in hospitality ever since. I picked him up because he's quick on his feet, and he's got my back. He's my apprentice—and my right hand for this trip."

Reed gave a shy but polite smile. "Hi, ladies. It's an honor to meet y'all. Harry's told me a lot about you—and believe me, he talks a lot."

Citrine squinted playfully. "You cook?"

Reed grinned, relaxing a little. "Yes, ma'am. And no offense, but British food ain't exactly Cajun-level. So if we need to whip something up while we travel, I got you."

Laughter rolled through the group. Even Moons chuckled softly.

Harry nodded proudly. "See? The man's got skills."

Aster caught Reed's eye and gave him a shy smile. He returned it, cheeks faintly pink. I pretended not to notice.

Harry went on, "Reed's still learning the ropes, but he's good people. He's got my back, and yours, too."

After introductions, Harry led us toward the passenger pick-up area. Peridot and Moons linked arms, trading stories about their military adventures while stationed in England.

That's one thing I wish I'd done before I was discharged: to live in Europe for a while.

Harry stopped in front of a slick passenger van. He cleared his throat to grab our attention. Citrine held my hand and squeezed. Deep down, I was excited to be on this trip. Citrine, Harry, now Aster on this trip? Along with Peridot and Moons? Europe better be on its heels when they saw us coming through.

"Hello, ladies. Let's get on the van so we can get to our destination. Your bags will meet us there." He gestured toward the door and we filed in and took our seats. Once everyone was inside and buckled, Harry got on the microphone and tapped it.

"Is this thing on? Perfect. Welcome, everyone. I'm Harry, your concierge for the duration of your trip. I'll be accompanying you to the following cities: London, UK; Brugge, Belgium; and Cologne, Germany. Maybe even Lille if we feel spicy. We'll play it by ear. If you need anything—spa day, sightseeing—let me know so I can arrange it. I've left the schedule free so you can explore and not look like a big tourist group. All I ask is that before you head out, please check in with me so I know where you are. Any questions?"

We all shook our heads. I knew the itinerary was going to be fabulous. After the corridor of sins, I needed something like this with my closest friends—my people.

Harry nodded, replaced the microphone, and took his seat. He motioned for the driver to take us to the next destination.

Citrine poked me. "So. What's first on the agenda?"

I shifted in my seat. "You know, after that long-ass flight, I need a nap."

Aster piped in. "Uh uh. No can do. Your body's got to get used to the time difference. I suggest we go get something to eat after we freshen up."

Citrine exchanged some dap with Aster, who was giggling. "That's my girl right there! Onyx, she's right. Let's freshen up and then grab something to eat. Once you get some good drink and food in your system, you'll be ready to go!"

I shrugged and sighed—in a good way. "Alright! Y'all twisted my arm!" I playfully rolled my eyes.

Harry jumped from the front to our row in one single bound, his eyes all bright with excitement. "Hey! So what's the word?"

Aster turned her eyes away. Then it clicked. They didn't know each other. "Aster, this is Harry. Harry, this is Aster. Harry played an important role in the takedown while I was on retreat in the Netherlands." I beamed as I watched them shake hands and exchange pleasantries.

"Now that we're all acquainted, what's the word?"

Citrine playfully threw him a look. "Dang, Harry! You get a promotion and now you think you get to be pushy?" We all laughed.

Peridot jumped in. "Hey, is the plan for just y'all or all of us?"

I swatted her hand. "Girl, you know you're invited no matter what! Stop acting brand new!" Peals of laughter filled the van. Even the driver smiled a little.

"Well," Aster began, "since Harry is our guide, why don't we follow his lead?"

All eyes were on Harry. "After we check in, we'll have an hour of downtime to unwind, refresh, write,"—he looked straight at me—"then we can go to either a curry house or a pub."

"Or both?" Moons whispered, trying not to set off an alarm.

Harry nodded. "Of course! Dinner and the pub or have dinner at a pub! Knock out two birds with one stone."

Unanimously, we voted for dinner at the pub. Harry gave us a thumbs-up and took his phone out of his pocket. He spoke briefly, then hung up.

"We're good. Oh snap! We're here."

We turned our heads and realized we were parked in front of a luxurious hotel with a park right across the street. As soon as we got off the van, the doorman greeted us and escorted us inside. The lobby was perfection. Marble floors glistened under crystal chandeliers. Velvet seating invited you to stay a while. Golden holiday garlands draped over polished railings, filling the air with a subtle scent of pine and spice.

If the rest of our trip was like this, well… damn.

Harry and Reed stepped up to the front desk. Harry leaned in to chat with the concierge, while Reed stayed close, scanning the lobby with calm vigilance. A moment later, Harry picked up a package. Together, he and Reed opened it, revealing a stack of key cards.

Harry turned back to us. "Alright, ladies. Here's the scoop. You're all sharing one grand suite—but with private rooms for each of you."

"Hold up," I said, hand raised, "is the whole floor a suite?"

Harry nodded and handed everyone a key. "Of course, ladies! Why is that even a question?"

We grabbed the keys and briskly walked to an available elevator. Then we stopped. We flipped the keys over, searching for room numbers.

***

Harry, with as much swagger as possible, sashayed onto the elevator and pressed the floor number.

He then turned and looked at us. "Next time, you will wait until I finish all instructions." He stuck out his tongue and, with dramatic flair, faced the elevator doors.

Reed just shook his head.

We all burst out laughing, even Moons with her mouselike chuckle.

***

After napping for forty-five minutes, my phone chimed with a text from Harry:

"Dinner at the pub. We'll leave in twenty minutes."

Damn. Didn't anyone believe in taking their time?

I jumped out of the tub and quickly got dressed. After one last look in the mirror, I blew a kiss at my reflection, grabbed my purse and jacket, and headed out.

As always, I was the last to arrive—but at least I wasn't late.

✳✳✳

We arrived at the pub and took our seats. Dinner was amazing. All that stuff I'd heard about bland British food? Not true tonight.

After the meal, we finished off our pints and drifted separately to other corners of the pub. Peridot and Moons decided to play some darts. Aster, Citrine, and Reed gathered at a table, deep in conversation. I wandered over to an unoccupied corner with my pint, needing a moment to myself.

"Whew!" Harry said, pretending to wipe sweat from his brow. Like magic, a server appeared with a pint of stout for Harry and a pint of cider for me. We gulped down our drinks as if we hadn't tasted anything in hours.

"So, Ms. Ma'am. How are you really doing?" Harry looked at me, his eyes full of concern.

I sighed as I stared at my now empty glass, wondering if I should order another round.

Harry placed his hand over mine. "Hey, it's me. You don't need another one." His gentle smile set my heart at ease.

I took a breath and dived in.

"I still have nightmares. I replay the scene with Raven over and over in my mind. But it's not just my mind—it's like I'm

121

reliving it. When I was placed on leave for a month, I saw her and Emerald every day."

Harry covered his mouth, tears welling in his eyes. "I'm so sorry. That must've been traumatic for you." He waved down a server for another round.

"I don't want you to feel sorry for me. I'm not saying all this so you'll pity me."

Harry waved me off. "I know you don't want to be coddled. But you need to know you've got people rooting for you, and you're not alone." He leaned over and wiped away a tear.

I leaned back in my chair and caught sight of Aster and Reed cuddled in a corner booth sharing appetizers and glasses of soda. She glowed.

"Anyway," I started again, "we were given a team assignment and honestly, I learned a lot about the world."

Harry took another sip of beer. "How so?"

Just as I was about to open my mouth, Citrine came over with Peridot and Moons. "Sorry to crash the party, but I know you weren't about to tell the story about La Dama Roja and the den of iniquity, were you?" She plopped into a chair, smiling from ear to ear. Yep—she was toasty.

I laughed as I took another sip. "Look. I need you to add anything I missed!"

Peridot's eyes were wide. "Den of iniquity? The fuck were y'all doing?" She sat straight up while Moons wrapped her hands around her pint, pale gaze fixed on me.

I took another deep breath and launched into the odyssey of La Dama Roja/La Puerta Obscura, leaving out the delicate parts of the Whisper Room, the Blue Room, and the Pride Room. Reed and Aster came over, grabbed seats, and listened. Citrine punched in highlights, carefully omitting classified details.

After we sang for our supper, everyone decided it was time to get back to the suite and call it a night.

✱✱✱

The next morning, I woke up refreshed. I slipped the sleek earbud into my ear. "Good morning, Crystal."

"Good morning, Commander. How was the flight last night? From what I could tell, your emotions came in waves – which isn't necessarily a bad thing."

"Yes, there were some somber moments, but it was all good for the most part."

"Glad to hear. Let's do a morning check-in."

"Fire away."

We went over my body and mental analysis. So far, it matched how I was feeling.

"Thanks for this, Crystal. We need to do this more often."

"How about first thing in the morning and last thing in the evening? That would build consistency."

"Sure. We've got to start somewhere, and if we need to adjust, that would allow flexibility."

"Thought of that by yourself, huh?"

"Crystal. Why are you starting first thing this morning?"

"Another part of the check-in. If you didn't respond back in the appropriate sense, I'd know something was off."

"That's pretty clever. Thought of that yourself, eh?"

"Touché, Commander. Touché."

"Well, I've got to get ready. Can you play my Christmas playlist?"

"Christmas playlist coming right up."

Right on cue, Good King Wenceslas played in my ear. I didn't know why I loved this song so much. Could be the story, how he cared for his page, how he helped the homeless man— or the composition itself.

A knock sounded on my door. Before opening it, I lowered my voice. "Crystal—go dark."

"Understood, Commander."

***

Feeling breezy, I skipped to the door and saw it was Aster. She looked comfortable in black slacks, a purple turtleneck, and her signature silver jewelry.

I invited her in, and she plopped on the bed.

"Hey friend! Ready for Belgium?"

"Oh yeah! I stayed up last night researching what I might want to get while we're there. As long as I get some Belgian chocolate and pastries, I'll be good!"

Aster leaned closer. "So… how's Crystal working?"

I sat beside her and lowered my voice. "Girl, I'm so happy I have her. She's the companion I needed. Especially during the last assignment."

Aster nodded. "I heard your briefing went well. I'm glad she worked out. But…" she dropped her voice lower, "I've got an update for you and Crystal."

"Talk to me."

"Girl… the analysis from your assignment has the higher-ups shaking. It's got me pulled onto another project already."

My pulse jumped. "What other project?"

She grimaced. "That I can't say. But I will say this: you and your team are about to go for a ride sooner than you think. Y'all are headed back into the field."

I sat back on my palms, my mind spinning. Part of me welcomed it. Another part wondered if I was ready. But hell… me and my team uncovered this mess. We should have first dibs on seeing it through.

Aster handed me a small thumb drive. "This is Crystal's update. Plug it in before you reach the last destination. Once it's uploaded, throw the thumb drive in some water. Then throw it away."

I took the drive from her and slipped it into my bra—safe, discreet, and close to the skin. Then I removed the earpiece and pressed it back into the fob. No open comms during transit; orders were orders.

We hugged, like some kind of release. It wasn't comfort so much as understanding — a silent promise that we'd survive whatever waited next.

***

Another knock brought me back to the present. I didn't need the peephole.

"Come on in, Citrine."

Just as I thought, Citrine bounded in, her ringlets bouncing.

"Christmas Express is leaving in five minutes! Y'all ready?"

I slapped my thighs and jumped up. "Let's do this!"

Aster giggled and followed us out. As we walked toward the foyer, Citrine linked arms with Aster.

"So… Aster. What's up with you and Reed?"

Aster blushed so hard, her cheeks were practically beet red. "He's… very interesting."

"Is that code for something else?" Citrine chuckled.

"I think we might need to put a mistletoe over their heads pretty soon!" I couldn't help but join in.

We got to the foyer and saw Harry and Reed talking with Peridot and Moons. Moons looked every bit the Christmas spirit, a holly wreath crowning her dark hair and glittering under the lights. Peridot—Peri, as she insisted last night—matched her with a hair clip decorated in berries and ivy. Both wore cozy sweaters and jeans. Citrine and I wore our own sweaters and pom-pom hats with scarves, and fur-trimmed boots. We were one good-looking group.

Harry and Reed were equally impressive in sharp pea coats and jeans. We were all in the holiday spirit.

"Wow! We sure know how to clean up!" Harry clapped his hands together as Reed nodded silently, eyes still drifting to Aster.

"Alright, here's the itinerary," Harry continued. "We'll take the train from London to Brussels, switch to Brugge. Dinner and rest tonight. Tomorrow is Brugge all day—shopping and eating. Then we'll catch another train to Cologne, check into the hotel, and the next day… the grandest Christmas market y'all will ever experience!" He flung his arms wide, beaming.

"Yippee!" Reed bounced on his toes, clapping his hands together.

I burst out laughing, while Citrine wiped tears from her eyes. Peri shook her head, and Moons tried her best not to snort.

Harry shot Reed a sidelong look and smoothed his coat. "Ladies, if you'll follow me, we'll head to breakfast and then the station. Now, hand over your keys and make sure you've got all your personal effects. As always, don't worry about your luggage."

He held out his hand and we each dropped our keys into his palm. Harry passed them to Reed, who counted them carefully, nodded, and gathered up our luggage to transport separately.

"Reed will meet us at the breakfast spot. If you'll follow me…" Harry spun on his heel and strode toward the elevators.

We all exchanged glances, then mimicked Harry's dramatic turn and followed suit, laughter echoing off the marble walls.

***

The platform buzzed with chatter and the scent of diesel. As we stepped aboard, I pressed my chest to confirm the drive was still secured in my bra. Satisfied, I took my seat beside Citrine, put in my earbuds, and closed my eyes.

The train hummed beneath my feet, steady as a heartbeat. A quick glance around the car told me everyone was either sleeping or staring out the window. Now was as good a time as any to use the bathroom—and handle Crystal's update while I was at it.

In the bathroom, the walls rattled with every turn of the rails. I locked the door, pressed the drive into the key fob's side port, and watched the indicator flicker red to yellow—then green. I removed one earbud, pulled the earpiece from the fob, and slid it into place.

"Good morning, Crystal."

"Morning, Commander. Update is complete." Her voice was a half-octave lower now, smoother than molasses.

I dropped the drive into the sink and let the water run until it stopped blinking, then crushed it under my heel and flushed the pieces. No evidence, no retrieval. By the time we disembarked, the update was secure, the system clean, and comms calibrated for the next phase.

I slipped back into my seat without anyone noticing. Leaning back, I let the motion of the train do the rest.

✳✳✳

After a smooth Eurostar ride into Brussels Midi, Harry hustled us onto a local train for Brugge.

"Only an hour, ladies!" he promised.

The platform smelled of coffee and waffles. Before we knew it, we were gliding past the winter fields and brick villages on our way to Christmas magic.

We checked into our hotel, which had plenty of charm, even if it wasn't as grand as the one in London. The place smelled faintly of wood polish and cinnamon, and old brass chandeliers glowed warmly over polished tile floors. Our suite had four rooms tucked off a cozy shared sitting area with velvet chairs and lace curtains that framed the view of narrow cobbled streets below.

Citrine and I bunked together, while Peri and Moons shared another. Harry and Reed took one room, and Aster claimed the fourth, though she ended up crashing in ours, which we were totally fine with.

By that point, it was late in the day and none of us felt like venturing out, so we ordered dinner in: crispy Belgian frites, steaming bowls of mussels, and warm, flaky pastries dusted with powdered sugar. The smells filled the suite, making it feel like a little holiday hideaway. We decided to save the real exploring for the morning light.

Brugge welcomed us with gray clouds and open arms. Cobblestone streets wound between medieval buildings, the overcast sky casting a soft glow over the holiday lights strung everywhere. Vendor stalls packed the city square, overflowing with food, jewelry, and clothes. It was pure joy chatting with merchants, each one describing their wares with fierce pride.

By the time we regrouped, my arms were loaded with roasted nuts, chocolate, a Belgian stein, lace fans, a couple of Brugge shot glasses, and a keychain shaped like the city's famous belfry. Citrine cleaned up, hauling bags of nuts and chocolate. Aster kept her promise, collecting artisan breads and more chocolate. Peri had two bags stuffed with chocolate wine, liqueurs, and a few bottles of limoncello. Moons cradled bolts of lace and vibrant cloth she'd unearthed in a tiny boutique.

Harry and Reed had their work cut out for them as they hustled between shops, helping us juggle bags and boxes, grinning through the chaos like the seasoned pros they were.

As the sun slipped behind the medieval rooftops, we knew it was time to move on. Brugge had cast its spell on us, but Cologne—and whatever awaited us there—was calling.

CHAPTER 2

Before the Holiday Fades

The train glided into the station so smoothly, I barely felt it stop. We hustled off onto the platform, waiting for Harry and Reed to tell us what came next. Reed was first off the train, Harry close on his heels. While Reed took a headcount, Harry was on the phone, his expression shifting from tense to radiant. He nodded at Reed, who gestured for us to follow him.

We were met by the same sleek passenger van. We piled in, luggage stowed, and pulled away into the city streets. The van zoomed through Cologne but somehow everything outside seemed to slow. The Christmas lights cast a warm glow across shopfronts and cobbled streets. Even the world-famous cathedral loomed above the skyline like something out of a fairytale, fitting perfectly into the holiday wonderland.

I glanced at the crew. Faces were pressed to windows, eyes shining, lips parted with quiet oohs and aahs. Even Peri, who usually shared my nonexistent holiday spirit, looked spellbound. The van pulled up to a building that blended into the neighborhood—understated from the outside but clearly hiding some serious elegance.

Harry escorted us to the entrance and unlocked the door. Once inside, approving gasps filled the air. The townhouse wrapped us in warmth: the scent of roasting chestnuts and spiced mulled wine floated through the air. A woman stepped forward, holding a tray with beers and bottles of mineral water.

"Welcome to Hafenhaus," she said, her voice brisk yet warm. "My name is Kora, and I'll be your host for the next few days. If you need anything while you're in Cologne, please don't hesitate to ask me, or your tour guides can contact me about any special wishes."

She turned toward Harry and Reed, diving into a rapid, lively discussion in German.

Citrine nudged me with her elbow. "Come on."

We followed her through the house. In the kitchen, Peri and Moons were already exploring. A spread of sandwiches, juice, tea, and water waited on the counter. My stomach won the debate, and I grabbed a couple sandwiches and a bottle of water. Citrine pulled out her phone, searching for the Christmas market map. We all leaned in, plotting our route like generals planning a campaign.

Soon Harry, Reed, and Kora joined us in the kitchen. Harry clapped his hands for attention.

"Alright, ladies. Room assignments. Onyx, Citrine, Peri, and Moons—you're in the big room upstairs. Aster, you've got a single. Reed and I are sharing, and Kora has her own apartment on the lower level."

He lifted an eyebrow. "Now, the itinerary for tomorrow is simple: market, market… and market."

We were about to head out when Moons cleared her throat.

"Um… I know we're here for the markets, but… is there time to visit the Cathedral?"

Harry's grin lit up the entire kitchen. "Of course there is! Who else wants to come along?"

Always a sucker for gothic architecture, my hand shot up, Citrine's following instantly. Aster nodded with a quiet smile, while Peri rolled her eyes but ultimately gave in.

"That's everyone, Harry," Reed said with a shrug and a small, conspiratorial smile.

Harry clapped his hands together. Kora piped up. "Would you like a guided tour or prefer to wander on your own?"

Moons' eyes widened and gleamed. "Can we have a guided tour?" She glanced back at the rest of us for support.

"Sure," I agreed. I loved old buildings—and how often do you get the chance to explore one of Europe's most famous cathedrals with a personal guide?

Peri stepped forward and wrapped an arm around Moons. "Maybe we can see that first… then go shopping? And eating? And drinking?"

I burst out laughing at Peri's list, punctuated with dramatic pauses. Aster joined me, chuckling, while Citrine's curls bounced as she bobbed her head in agreement.

Harry looked at Kora with anticipation. Kora strolled over to the house phone and spoke rapid German. She hung up and gave instructions to Reed.

✳✳✳

The Cologne Cathedral was spectacular. The stained-glass windows, the pews, even the altar—it was nothing short of breathtaking. We finished the tour and stepped into the sunshine, the spires stretching above us toward the heavens.

The group gathered and started walking toward the markets. I drifted behind, lost in my own thoughts. I was halfway through mapping out my next poetry collection inspired by the cathedral when a light tap on my shoulder snapped me back to reality. Moons stood beside me, eyes shining. Damn. Don't that girl make any noise?

Moons smiled shyly as she inched closer. "Didn't you feel the spirit of past lives and ceremonies living in there?"

I made a mental note to connect her with Lotus—Moons carried that same down-to-earth, spiritual vibe. I linked my arm through hers and rested my head against her shoulder. "Now that you mention it… yeah. I felt a calm in there. I'm glad we listened to you and took the tour."

Moons leaned closer and dropped her voice to a whisper. "When was the last time you communed with your protector?"

The question stopped me cold. To be honest, I hadn't saluted Oya, the Orisha of storms and winds, in a long time. Life had been chaos and my devotion slipped through the cracks.

I ducked my head. "It's been a while."

She grinned, like she was in on some secret. "Listen. When we're all having drinks, pour a shot for your protector. Go outside, find earth, water, or fire—and pour it out. Give her thanks."

I squeezed her arm. Somehow, her words grounded me. She leaned in, and I felt her energy humming through my body.

We visited every stall in the center market. Citrine picked out Christmas decorations for the house, while the rest of us stocked up on jewelry, scarves, and all manner of treats. The excitement buzzed like electricity through the crowds.

Together, we decided to get gifts for Harry, Reed, and Kora as a thank you for being such excellent hosts. We had to sneak around so they wouldn't catch on.

We'd just finished our shopping and were deciding whether to go for lunch or dinner when Citrine suddenly gasped.

"Oooh! Look at the river and the bridge in the background! We have to take a picture!" She grabbed my sleeve and dragged me toward the railing, shoving her phone into Peri's hands.

"Quick! Take the picture before she changes her mind!"

I chuckled as I stood in position. "I don't hate pictures, I just hate how I look in them."

Peri waved me off. "Girl, hush! Do you not know how stunning you look?"

Citrine chimed in. "That's what I told her! Not to mention the many dudes who stopped in their tracks and gawked at her as she walked past oblivious!"

My cheeks warmed even in the cold air. They sure knew how to make a girl feel good about herself.

Peri snapped our photo. Then Citrine waved Aster into the frame for another picture.

Harry and Reed approached, both carrying mugs of mulled wine. Peri spotted them and thrust the phone at Harry.

"You *know* I need a picture!" Peri dashed into the frame, crouching low in a pose straight out of a prison yard. Snap! Another photo.

I looked around and spotted Moons lingering at the edge of the group. "Moons!" I called. "If you don't get your free-spirited ass in this photo—"

Moons giggled and scampered over, squeezing in beside Peri. The group shot came out perfect.

As we debated what to do next, a tall, wiry woman with pale blond hair and pale eyes approached. Her presence was delicate and a little awkward but somehow striking. She offered to take a picture of all of us—including Harry and Reed.

Harry thanked her and practically shoved Reed into the group shot while he pranced around. Harry stopped, spun, and struck a dramatic pose. "I was beginning to wonder if y'all heifers were gonna let us in the picture!"

"No one would or could forget about adding you to anything!" I shot back. Laughter echoed as the woman snapped the picture.

She handed Citrine her phone and smiled politely. "You all look like you're having such a great time."

We all agreed, voices overlapping.

She continued, her tone slipping into crisp professionalism. "Allow me to introduce myself. My name is Io. I'm with the DS Office here in Germany. I'm here to escort you to our office for an important assignment."

Damn. Seriously?

CHAPTER 3

The Moment the Lights Went Out

While we were following Io, a couple of questions flooded my mind. Before I could speak, Peri jumped the gun and spoke. She stopped Io and turned her around to face us.

"First off, hi. How you doing?" Peri waited for an answer with her arms folded. Moons tried to stifle a laugh.

Io stared back with a blank stare. "I'm good. This way please." She turned back around. Peri spun her back.

"Why the hell did you wait to tell us who you were? What made you think it was a good idea to drop a bomb like that on us, knowing we here on vacation and having a good ol' time?" She stood back with hands on hips and lips pursed.

The rest of us were wondering the same thing and I was mentally thanking Peri. She said it exactly how I would've said it. My eyes darted to Citrine; I could tell she was thinking the same thing. Aster looked more amused.

Io cast her eyes down. "I'm sorry for the abruptness but I was told to get you all by any means possible."

Harry stepped forward, standing closer to her while still giving her space. "Is it okay if I place my hand on your shoulder?"

She nodded.

"Does it matter where?" he asked.

She shook her head.

He slowly and gently placed his hand on her left shoulder. "What you did was very brave. We appreciate you letting us know and guiding us to where we need to be. We're not mad, just overwhelmed and concerned." He removed his hand and stepped back.

Io released a tiny smile but still didn't look up. "Thank you for the reassurance. I guess it can be confusing, especially if you haven't met or seen me before." She turned around, starting to walk, and we followed towards a row of buildings.

As we power-walked, I heard Peri whispering to Harry. "What was that all about?" she tried to whisper, but it was more like a hoarse croak.

Harry whispered back. "I think she may be autistic. I've got a sister who shows the same traits. I took a gamble."

"Boy, I feel like an asshole," murmured Peri, exhaling as her eyes softened.

"Don't feel that way. The thing about autism is they still want independence. Don't baby or coddle them. In fact, she probably felt part of the group when you talked to her like that.

The only thing is… she couldn't tell if you were mad, sad, or anything. Which is why it didn't bother her."

We crossed streets and kept walking. Man, she was hard to keep up with. Even on a side street, the city still looked festive with boughs of holly and twinkling lights. Io kept her head down as she quickened her pace. She stopped in front of a nondescript building. We tried not to crowd her as she punched in the code. The door hissed open, and she motioned for us to follow her down a dark hallway.

I whispered to Harry as we descended. "Is this safe?"

"This is the DS building in Germany. Normally, this is the training center for our hospitality cells in Europe. But I wonder why they're bringing y'all here?"

I wondered the same myself as we entered a conference room. On the big screen, I saw Sid, Pearl, Ruby, and another person I didn't recognize.

Peri eased into her seat and turned to Moons. "Hey, why's our boss here?"

Moons shrugged. "Don't know, but whatever the reason, it must be important."

Citrine spun in her seat to face Peri. "Who's that?"

Moons lowered her voice. "That's Malachi. He's head of me and Peri's section—Walnut. Who's that?" She pointed at Pearl.

"That's Pearl. She's Citrine's and my boss. She's in charge of Cashew."

Then it dawned on me. Walnut is the Special Victims section. If Moons and Peri work for Malachi, then they belong to Special Victims. I'd heard that's our no-killing unit. If the perpetrator's on the extermination list, they hand them over to us.

"So wait a minute," Peri interrupted my train of thought, "if you're with Cashew, that means you've killed people?" Lord knows she tried to whisper but once again it came out like a hoarse croak.

Citrine looked at her. "Indeed."

Peri looked impressed while Moons covered her mouth, her eyes wide.

Moons glanced at the screen again. "Who's the other person?"

"That is Ruby. Director of HR and second in command," a voice boomed from the rear.

We all whirled in our seats and saw an older woman briskly walking into the room. Kora was right behind her. I loved the outfit: a white polka-dot top with a navy blue pencil skirt and sensible shoes. Her makeup was flawless.

"Hello, everyone. I know this meeting is cutting your vacation short, and I do apologize. However, something serious has come up to where we need all your talents."

She scanned the room as she handed some tablets to Io. Kora took her place right next to Harry and Reed. Harry gave her a look, and Kora mouthed, "I didn't know."

Opal continued. "You've met Io, my assistant and cousin. She's the administrative assistant and doesn't do operative work. She wanted to help, so I asked her to gather you all. I hope she didn't startle you."

"Not at all. She took a great picture of us before she escorted us here," Peri said as she pulled up the photo.

Opal smiled and gave Io a thumbs up. Io returned the gesture. The way they interacted warmed my heart.

Opal signaled for Io to unmute the mic. As soon as she saw she was live, she began.

"We've had a situation that's been brewing for some time. Unfortunately, this situation has crossed over to multiple sections and requires immediate attention." She clicked her pointer, and there were two photos: a female in a Navy uniform, and a male in a Marine uniform.

"Meet HM3 Whitney Taggert and Cpl Benjamin Lancaster. Both were stationed near Stuttgart. Both have been described as hardworking and dedicated. According to sources, they recently disappeared a few days after attending a party."

Citrine and I exchanged looks while Peri and Moons had the same expression—WTF and I know you lying. Opal noticed and spoke.

"Do you know them already?"

"No," I said, "but the circumstances are familiar." The rest murmured in agreement.

Peri piped up. "Let me guess: no one knows anything and they won't talk?"

Opal pointed to her nose as Malachi spoke up. "We were investigating something similar." He looked through his notes. "Here it is. A Senior Airman Phillips. We took down her story and everything."

Moons nodded. "Yes. She was prepared to give her statement and everything. Even with everything going on, she remained strong. Then, suddenly, she disappeared. We eventually found her but she refused to talk to us."

Ruby shook her head as Sid chimed in. "Well, this case definitely belongs in our wheelhouse, but I don't understand how this fell into our lap in the first place."

Pearl spoke up. "During our staff meeting, Malachi, Opal, and I were talking. We compared notes and Opal said a family member works with Hospital Corpsman Third Class Taggert. Apparently, they usually meet for breakfast and one day, she just didn't show. When her supervisor was asked, they said she's on extended leave. It's been thirty days and still no word. So," Pearl gulped, "I think all our high-priority cases are tied in somehow."

Sid nodded. "Now it makes sense. So the question is: what do we do?"

Ruby drummed her fingers together, brows furrowed. "No extermination orders at this time. The job is recon. Are the associates in the room capable of this task?"

Sid was about to speak, but Malachi cut her off. "Peri and Moons are the best in my division. Years of experience between them. I wouldn't trust anyone else with this but them."

Pearl took over the conversation. "And you know who my people are."

Ruby smirked. "Yes, I know who they are. They handled the La Dama Roja case. Sid, thoughts?"

Sid took her glasses off. "I stand with both my chiefs. Try to find anyone better. You won't."

Harry snapped his fingers while Kora and Reed looked over at us with smiles.

"Well," Ruby said as she sat back in her chair, "I will bring this up to Glacier and see what she says. It is ultimately up to her. Before I do, how do the agents feel? Are they willing to do it? Opal, if they choose to pursue this and they're cleared, do we have the support?"

Opal cast glances to Harry, Reed, and Kora. Harry gave her a thumbs up. "We stand ready to assist them in any way we can."

Everyone looked at us. All the girls looked at me. For a second, I thought, *Why this shit on me?* However, I was the legend who uncovered the plot and survived seven corridors of sin. I cleared my throat.

"We're the best. Let's show whoever's behind this why."

Pearl, Malachi, and Sid nodded while Ruby clapped her hands. "It's settled then. Stand by until you hear from me. It should be no later than tomorrow morning. In the meantime, prepare as if you are going. Any questions?"

We all shook our heads.

"That concludes this meeting. See you all tomorrow." Ruby clicked off the conference, followed by the rest.

No one said a word for what seemed like a long time. Opal stood and faced us.

"Thank you all so much for doing this. I know you're on vacation, but—"

Citrine held up her hand. "No need to apologize. This is what we do. Aster," she turned, "can you work as an analyst in a pinch since we don't have our team locally?"

Aster grinned broadly. "Absolutely."

While everyone was making plans, the room was spinning. I'd just somewhat recovered from the last assignment, and now we were plunging into this? Why did I always plunge into assignments? Why couldn't I be eased into one?

I leaned over to Opal and asked for the restroom.

She said no problem and that Io could show me. Io waved over at me and walked in the direction on her tiptoes. She pointed to the door. I thanked her and went inside. Luckily, it was a single toilet. I locked the door, used the bathroom, washed my hands, and splashed some cold water on my face. I sighed.

"Crystal? Are you there?" I asked as I made sure the water remained running.

"Yes, Commander. Are you alright? Your heart rate has jumped significantly."

"No, Crystal. I—"

"Just breathe, Commander. Take your time."

I did as instructed and I began to see clearer.

Crystal came back on. "You were having a panic attack. I pinpointed when your heart rate jumped, and it was when it was announced you're on another mission."

"Yeah, a no-kill assignment. Damn!"

"Careful. What's the problem?"

I blew out a puff of air. "I finally get a chance to let my hair down, and now this! Seriously?"

"I know it's frustrating, Commander. But what if they'd chosen someone else? What if they didn't even consider you? You'd be angry instead of feeling overwhelmed."

Crystal was right. Something like this, especially after what I've been through, would've been a slap in the face if they chose someone else.

I stared into the mirror. "But why does the weight have to be on my shoulders?"

"Do you not want it to be?"

I blinked. I really didn't know what I wanted. Crystal spoke again.

"Out of everyone here, you are the most seasoned besides Citrine. Let Citrine handle the logistics and you two collaborate. At the end of the day, it goes through you."

"But how do I lead them? I barely know them."

Crystal's stern voice rang in my ear. "Then get to know them. To lead, you must know. And if you need help, I'm here."

I smiled and mouthed *thank you*. Then Crystal piped in. "They're looking for you. You need to head back."

I shut off the water and left. I walked down the hallway and Io came from around the corner.

"Hello, Onyx."

"Hey, Io. Just on my way back."

"I figured," she said as she played with her fidget spinner. "Who were you talking to?" She stopped fidgeting and stared at me.

Shit. She heard me talk to Crystal. "I was talking to myself. I sometimes do that to figure things out."

Her eyes widened. "Me too! I'm so glad I'm not the only one. You name your friend Crystal. I name mine Jordan. After my mom."

"That's sweet." I really needed to be careful. I thought the water drowned my voice.

"Anyway," Io said, "ready to go? I can show you the way."

"Awesome! Let's go!"

She grabbed my hand and squeezed. I squeezed her hand back. Then we skipped back to the conference room… as if my vacation wasn't just completely ruined.

CHAPTER 4

The Weight of Silence

The ride back to the house was quiet. You could hear a mouse piss on a ball of cotton. The van stopped in front of Hafenhaus and everyone tumbled out. After Kora unlocked the door, Peri dashed inside and went straight to the bathroom. I heard a sigh of relief through the bathroom door. Dang, she must've held it for quite some time.

Moons waltzed in while Citrine and Aster barreled through the door. Harry, Reed, and I were the last to come in. I took off my coat, hat, and gloves and hung them in the closet before heading straight to the kitchen, opening up cabinets.

Harry's face scrunched up in a frown. "Ma'am, what do you think you're doing?" He placed his hands on his hips.

Reed chimed in. "Harry! Don't you know the behavior of a woman who was just handed some heavy news? She wants a drink, and not the ones that tickle. Am I right?"

"Absolutely," I said as I kept looking. Reed came up behind me and placed his hand on mine. "You don't have to do everything on your own." His eyes matched his smile.

I nodded and sat down at the table. Reed found a tumbler and the liquor. He poured me a whiskey. He put down a napkin and placed my drink on top, finishing with a flourish.

I lifted an eyebrow. "How'd you know I like my whiskey neat?"

Reed's cheeks were flushed. "You filled out a dossier on your favorite things including your drink. I just assumed this is what you wanted."

I grinned. "It was. Thank you." I took the drink and sipped slowly.

Peri came down the stairs. "They've got to be fucking kidding me! Why bring us in if y'all already didn't have the clearance? I'd rather you tell me we were assigned instead of telling us we might be assigned and have us sit on pins and needles for a fucking answer!"

She clasped her hands and started to rub them. I mentally made a note that when Peri was anxious and ticked off, she paced, wrung her hands, and lashed out. I did appreciate seeing how she handled situations so I knew her limits.

Moons came into the kitchen and made some tea. She poured some for Peri and herself. When Moons handed Peri a tea cup, her stance went from defensive to calm. She sipped some tea, mumbled an apology, and went outside.

Moons drank her tea and sighed. "In a way, I don't blame her. Why bring this to our attention if they have no idea if we're going to do this? The attitude shifted in a not-so-good way." She got up and followed Peri out of the room.

I swirled my glass, looking at the amber liquid. Harry nodded while Reed refilled my glass. Citrine walked into the room.

"Hey Reed. Can I get one of those?"

Reed smiled. "Coming right up." He grabbed another glass and poured some whiskey. He handed it to Citrine as she sat right next to me.

"Why do I get the feeling the party we went to and this incident are linked?" She stared off as Aster joined us.

Reed blushed, jumped up, and fixed Aster some tea and croissants with jam.

Reed was so red, I thought he was a strawberry. "Here Aster. I made you some tea with cream, some croissants, and some local jams: rose hip and red currant. One sweet and one tart. Enjoy."

Harry and I exchanged looks while Citrine smiled. "Dang, Reed! What service! Too bad the rest of us didn't receive the red carpet treatment!"

That statement, followed by peals of laughter, was just enough to break up the tension we all were feeling. I loved my partner, especially in these moments.

Just then, Kora came in with groceries. "After what just happened, I figured I'd fix dinner tonight."

Harry beamed as the rest of us clapped. "Splendid! Would you like some help?"

"Indeed, I would," said Kora as she unloaded the groceries.

"What's on the menu?" asked Citrine after she swallowed her sip and leaned forward.

Kora flashed a smile. "Some Rheinischer Sauerbraten with Himmel un Aad. And for dessert: Vanillekipferl." She giggled to herself.

I scanned the room and figured everyone was thinking the same thing, so I decided to speak up. "Sounds delicious! What is it?"

Without missing a beat, Kora continued. "Slow roasted beef with a sweet and sour gravy made with raisins, and mashed potatoes with an apple compote. For dessert, in honor of the holiday, I'm making some delicious slices of heaven—or some vanilla shortbread cookies." She was ecstatic about making us dinner as she giggled to herself again.

While Kora and Harry made dinner, and Reed attended to Aster, Citrine and I started to talk about today's events. Crystal buzzed me in my ear. "Glacier needs to talk with you alone. Be ready in two minutes."

To not arouse suspicion, I created a diversion. "Hey Kora. Do we have breakfast coming tomorrow or— "

Kora jumped up. "I can order something." She pulled up her tablet. "What would you all like?"

Everyone started to shout everything at her. She typed furiously to keep up with the demand. As they were busy getting specifics for breakfast, I slipped out of the room to take Glacier's call.

My phone vibrated. I ducked into a room and locked the door.

"Onyx, I wanted to discuss this assignment with you personally. I heard everything from Ruby and Sid, but I need your opinion."

I leaned against a wall. "My professional opinion or my honest opinion?"

Glacier chuckled. "Whiskey straight."

"These disappearances appear to be connected. It would help us know who we're up against if we investigate." Glacier sighed heavily, which was out of character for her. Usually, she was decisive, hence her name —ice cold in every part of her life. "Look, this could unravel something we may not be able to control."

"Wouldn't it be better to know anyway? If we investigate and find something, then you can make an informed decision on next steps." I countered and held my breath. The hairs on the back of my neck stood up. Something was off and it didn't feel right.

I heard Glacier shift in her seat. She then lowered her voice. "You're right. Let's find out everything if this case is connected to the other cases we have. Work this one off the books. Y'all have the ability to do that. You have nine days to complete the investigation. Any more time, it'll tip people off. If you all get caught, you're on your own. If you agree with that, you may proceed with the investigation."

I clamped my hand over my mouth to keep from screaming. "I'm sure they'll agree with that. What about Harry and Reed?"

"They will follow protocol. Ruby already gave them their orders. Here are mine: work it, but off the books."

"And who do we report to with our findings?"

"Sid. Report to Sid. I'll let her know the deal."

I took a deep breath. I'd done clandestine, off-the-record assignments before, but without support. What did I just agree to?

"Sounds good. Thank you for believing in us."

"And thank you for believing in the mission. Talk soon." And with that, she hung up.

As the coldness of the wall helped center me, my mind was scrambled. Why were we working off the table? Why was Glacier hesitant to approve this? Why ask me?

I shook my head and left the room to rejoin the group.

After that call from Glacier, I knew whatever decision made would have implications on everything we knew. For the moment, everyone either stayed in their room or found a corner for solace. Couldn't say I blamed them since our whole trip had turned upside down.

I needed something to drink, so I went down the stairs into the kitchen. Harry was humming to himself at the kitchen table while Reed had his earbuds on, watching something on his tablet. They both acknowledged me but I knew it was out of formality, not necessity. I poured myself a drink and looked out the window. The backyard, small as it was, looked marvelous with the snow against the gray sky. Then I saw Peri, pacing as she smoked a cigarette. Why in the world was she out there? It was freezing.

I put my cup down and started to look around for two blankets. Harry looked up and left the room. He returned promptly with two mink throws and handed them to me.

"All you had to do was ask." He smiled at me.

"I asked through my body language," I said as I winked and gave him a peck on the cheek.

He grinned as he shook his head. I put on one of the throws and went outside. Peri didn't even hear me, so when I tapped her, she jumped.

"Jesus!" she exclaimed as she put out her cigarette. "Where did you come from?"

"From the kitchen. I saw you out here and just wanted to make sure you're okay." I handed her a throw and took a seat on one of the chairs in the backyard.

She put it on, relief washing over her face. "Thank you for this. I wanted to get one but I didn't want to leave. For some reason the cold is also comforting."

"I get it. When I'm in the middle of a smoke session, I want to finish it."

She nodded and looked away. "What do you think is going to happen?"

I shrugged. "It's hard to say. As long as it's the right thing. But I didn't come out here to talk shop. I wanted to get to know you. Since we've been on this trip, we haven't really had any alone time to get to know each other."

She threw her head back, her laugh echoing off the house. "Is this your way of getting to know me? You don't have to do the textbook formalities."

"I can respect that. So, what's your story?"

Peri lit another cigarette. "Do you mind?"

"Not at all."

She took a puff and blew it out. The corners of her mouth turned up. "Recently retired from the military. I joined because I reached out to Glacier to investigate the disappearance of my sister and her friend. My sister was my best friend." Her voice slowed from quick beats to a quiet, even cadence.

"Her so-called friends murdered her and her friend. Over some dude. When I discovered the reason, I took out one of the girls before Glacier and her team executed the plan. She showed up at my sister's funeral, chastised me, then recruited me."

It always seemed as if there had to be some sort of tragedy involved for anyone to join this organization. I guess it provided motive but damn, we were nothing but a bunch of tragic figures trying to make up for it by rehabilitating or exterminating perpetrators. I sighed.

Peri stopped and looked at me. "I know it's heavy, but you wanted to know."

I nodded. "This is true. I ain't mad at how you're telling me these things. So, what's your position?"

She put out the cigarette. "I investigate crimes. That's how y'all get your assignments and the data. We do the groundwork: research, analysis, interviews, advocacy work for the victims."

I could tell by the furrowed brows and the faraway look, she was thinking about her sister. I had to ask. "Have you killed anyone?"

She shook her head. "Almost. It scared me. I could never do what you do." She turned to look at me. "How do you deal with it?"

"I have a very strong support system. Not gonna lie, it does bother me sometimes. But who I exterminate deserved it."

"You think so? I mean, we've all heard how you took out Venom. That was pure hatred, especially involving her kids."

"She orchestrated my rape and the rape of other women as well. If she saw you as a threat, that's what she did. Hers is the only one I don't regret."

Peri mulled it over. "That's fair and I understand. So you're not bloodthirsty?"

"Of course not! That's how I handle it."

A throat cleared behind us. We whipped around to see Kora blowing into her hands. "Ladies, hate to interrupt, but we got an answer. Follow me, please."

Peri and I exchanged looks as we got up. Peri stopped me. "Thanks for the talk. I feel better with you being our leader. I hope I can contribute to the level you expect."

I gave her a hug. "From the files I've read on you, you are more than capable." I gestured for her to walk inside and I followed after.

Everyone was crowded in the kitchen/dining room, huddled around the tablet with Sid. The room felt stuffy with anxiety as we awaited the answer.

"Hello, everybody. I'm glad everyone's here. We are go for the assignment. However, this is off the record. You're on your own publicly. If something happens and you get caught, we won't be able to help. But you have access to everything we have here to accomplish this. Kora, Harry, and Reed have agreed to stay on to help support. Peri will investigate while

Moons will provide victim advocacy support and mental health for the team. Aster will compile Peri's notes and produce a product for Citrine and Onyx, who will follow up on any leads. They will report to me. You all have a two-week deadline for this, then you will be pulled. If you finish in under two weeks, the better. This is a recon-only mission. Do you agree to the terms?"

The team exchanged looks and then looked at me, nodding their heads.

"Sid, we agree and we're prepared."

Sid clapped her hands. "Excellent. Good luck to you all and looking forward to hearing from you soon." Just like that, she disconnected.

Everyone but Citrine and I left the room. I looked at Citrine. "It feels off—like someone doesn't want us to be involved. And that makes me want to dig deeper."

Citrine's lips curved in a wry smile. "That's why we work so well together."

"Agreed. No need to alarm the rest until we have concrete evidence. Which Peri and Moons can provide. Once we get their notes, we can go over them with Aster."

Citrine nodded. "Well then. We've got a plan. In the meantime, let's see how dinner turned out and if Kora and Harry need help with the meal." She gulped her last drop and headed toward the door.

I followed her out with my glass, ready to devour the meal Kora and Harry prepared.

CHAPTER 5

Unraveling the Ties that Bind

After wrapping up our holiday spirit and getting the green light from Sid, we moved quickly but cautiously. We only had two weeks—and we were off the record. Peri and Moons interviewed associates and possible victims of the two missing service members, while Aster created a virtual database to keep notes and evidence together and stored.

Harry, Reed, and Kora were godsends. They made sure we were fed and had our laundry washed, and drove us anywhere we needed to go. Citrine and I followed up on leads whenever Peri and Moons passed along intel.

We all agreed work and where we were staying should stay separate, so we worked out of the DS building and keep Hafenhaus as our refuge.

***

Citrine and I walked in three hours before we were to brief Sid. To our surprise, Opal and Io were setting up the conference room. Aster joined them, hooking up the database to the equipment for our briefing. Harry and Reed arrived with everyone's breakfast orders. They also set up coffee, juice, and tea.

I looked in the basket and saw the cookies Kora made for our dinner last week. Those vanilla slices of heaven were delicious. Harry leaned over and whispered:

"Kora noticed you loved those cookies and made extra ones especially for you." He winked as I grabbed one and stuffed it in my mouth.

***

Once everything was ready, Citrine, Opal, Io, and I pulled up the notes.

Peri and Moons had interviewed several people connected to the two missing service members. Peri's report summarized it like this: About a month and a half ago, Cpl Benjamin Lancaster received an invite from one of his buddies about a party happening later that evening. Since Lancaster was new and didn't know anyone, he figured it'd be okay. As the party raged, his friends wondered where he was but assumed he'd left with a girl, so they went home.

A few hours later, Lancaster returned to the barracks, drunk, bloodied, and bruised. His friends tried to get him into his room so he could sleep it off, but he started to have a seizure. Panicked, they drove him to the military hospital and dropped him off. The graveyard crew stabilized him, and when he woke up, HM3 Whitney Taggert stitched him up. Lancaster told her about the party and how he'd gotten his bruises. Taggert reported it to the attending physician. The next day, both disappeared—and hadn't been seen since.

Moons' report noted they'd spoken with several close associates. One witness said something chilling: "Please make sure no one knows I spoke with y'all. People are disappearing if they talk about any of these parties. I don't want to die."

When Moons asked whether she believed Lancaster and Taggert were dead, the woman replied without hesitation. "Without a doubt. This isn't the first time—or the last."

Citrine added the financial piece. She and I had dug into finances and personnel records. We discovered several people connected to these events had bank accounts that were suddenly fatter than usual—and some had been promoted earlier than they should've been. One thing they all shared: they refused to talk any further.

After everything was added, Aster drew a map connecting the dots. Everything that happened here mirrored what happened at La Dama Roja. The only difference was the two missing service members.

"Aster," I said as I sipped my coffee, chomping another cookie, "see if there are any reported service members missing in or around the Complex."

Aster typed furiously. "Yes—this person here." She pulled up a picture of the same redhead who'd been escorted out of one of the rooms at La Puerta Obscura, which had prompted Citrine and me to follow her.

"She's Logistics Specialist First Class Brittany Towns. Her command reported her missing thirty days after the party you and Citrine went to."

Citrine grabbed a croissant and poured herself some coffee. "Aster, do we know any high-profile military people here locally who could've been at that party?"

Aster's fingers flew again. "There are a few," she said, flashing images of different officers, some familiar and some not. "However, the commander of the American Forces in Europe is the highest-ranking."

An image popped onto the screen.

I spat out my coffee while Citrine exclaimed, "Holy shit!"

The image was General Howard. He was the same guy we'd seen being pulled into the wall in the Anger corridor at La Puerta Obscura.

This was the connection. And judging by the bruises in the images, they mirrored the same ones we'd seen on that general. He had to be involved somehow.

Opal's eyes widened, her voice grave. "We've got to be real careful about this. That general holds a lot of power. This probably explains why everyone was so hesitant about this case."

I looked over at Opal while grabbing another cookie. "What do you suggest?"

Opal straightened her posture. "Relay the facts. Only the facts. Tie the pieces together if asked. Remember—this was a recon mission. There's a reason why it was recon."

A chime rang. Opal glanced up at the wall clock. "Five minutes before the briefing." Harry and Reed nodded. "We'll be in the other offices if you need us," Harry said. I nodded, and they briskly left.

Opal glanced at Io, who was finishing up on her tablet. "Io, why don't you help Harry and Reed figure out lunch since it's fast approaching?"

Io turned off her tablet. "Sure!" She pranced to the door on her tiptoes and shut it behind her.

Opal looked at us. "Just breathe, ladies. You got this."

A message alert popped up, signaling Sid was in the waiting room for the video call. Opal let her in and Sid's face appeared on the screen.

"Ladies, no formalities. What you got?"

We ran down everything we'd uncovered. The more we briefed, the more Sid's face turned to stone.

When we finished, Sid exhaled and addressed us. "Ladies, I don't have to tell you what this means. This is way bigger than we thought. I'll brief Glacier and figure out next steps. In the meantime, excellent work by the team. Y'all really didn't know each other, but you pulled it together. Expect a call from me later tonight. Anything else?"

No one said a word.

Sid nodded. "Good. Talk to you soon." She disconnected.

Tears streamed from Opal's eyes. "Does this mean... they're dead?"

Citrine and I didn't want to say anything—but we felt compelled to do so.

I sighed. "I hope not... but it's looking that way."

***

A buzz chirped in my ear.

"Commander, there's something urgent we need to discuss. Go to the bathroom."

Crystal had spoken urgently before—but never like this. I quickly excused myself and headed for the bathroom.

I shut the door and locked it.

"Talk to me, Crystal."

"I detected a signature pattern that doesn't belong here."

"What do you mean?"

"Everyone's signature pattern from DS checks against the roster. Only one isn't on the roster."

I blinked, trying to piece it together. "Who does the pattern belong to?"

"Quartz, Commander."

My heart paused. Why would Quartz be here? He wasn't German. He wasn't on this assignment. If anything, he should be working his regular job as an active-duty soldier. But he wasn't stationed anywhere near here.

"I'm locked in on everyone's footprint that you've come in contact with. However, a member of your team is here—but we weren't aware they should be here. Especially since we're working this assignment off the books."

My pulse thudded in my ears. Amethyst and Lotus communicated everything. But Quartz... he always did his own thing. Nobody ever questioned it. Maybe because everyone assumed someone else authorized it.

"Is it Quartz?"

"It is, Commander. Facial scan confirmed—biometric match through the local surveillance grid."

"Keep it quiet for now. Are you able to tail him?"

"Absolutely. His signal is already within range."

My stomach dropped. Quartz was supposed to be at the Complex. I knew for a fact he wasn't assigned to any cases. If Crystal was picking him up, either the mission had shifted without anyone knowing… or he'd gone rogue.

"Tail him. See where he goes. I'm curious myself."

"Copy all."

I let my head roll back. Great. Another thing I have to brief.

I splashed cold water on my face, trying to cool the emotion burning in my chest. I wiped my face dry, tossed the towel into the bin, and stared at my reflection.

Here we go again.

I unlocked the door and headed back to the others, feeling the weight of the secrets I now carried alone.

CHAPTER 6

The Invisible Trace

I returned to Hafenhaus, my thoughts spinning like a top. Why the fuck was Quartz here? He had no reason to be in Germany. I also wondered how I was going to tell Citrine what I know without exposing Crystal.

Fortunately enough, I got the breakthrough I needed.

Crystal chimed in my ear. "Commander, Quartz is moving."

I bolted upright. "Where?"

"The café nearest the Cologne Cathedral. He just arrived."

"Send me the coordinates."

My phone chimed, and I saw he was less than six minutes away.

I bounded down the stairs. Citrine, Aster, Harry, and Reed were playing cards. Citrine looked up. "Hey, Onyx! Where you going?"

"I'm craving those pastries from the café we visited after the cathedral tour."

Harry dropped his cards. "Oh my god, yes! That apple strudel is to die for!"

Citrine's curls bounced. "Girl! I know exactly which ones you're talking about! Can I come?" Before I could say anything, she dashed to the coat rack and threw on her coat and shoes. "I'll be back to finish whooping y'all's asses in a minute!"

We opened the door and Harry called after us. "Make sure you bring some of that apple strudel or we'll whoop that ass!"

Everyone laughed as we shut the door. I looked at my phone and followed the route. Within three minutes, Citrine started panting. "Damn, slow down! The café will still be there—it ain't going nowhere!"

I slowed my pace. "Sorry. It's cold and those pastries are calling my name."

"You damn right it's cold! In that case, let's pick up the pace!" Citrine tried to power walk but I caught up to her in no time. We both giggled at our silliness and linked arms.

We arrived in record time. Heavenly scents and the café owner welcomed us with open arms. As I looked over the rows of pastries, I felt a hard nudge in my ribs.

I turned to Citrine and mouthed "ow."

Citrine gestured with her eyes. I followed her gaze and saw Quartz, sitting in a booth, nursing a mug. His eyes kept darting between the mug and the street, as if he was expecting someone.

She grabbed our pastries and pulled me to a table a few paces behind him. We sat down where we could see him but he couldn't see us unless he was heading to the women's restroom.

I gave her a look and she shushed me. "Let's see who he's meeting first. Let the meeting happen. We'll have more information about what's going on and our next move."

I relented, and we waited. Suddenly, Quartz grabbed his phone and started to scroll.

Crystal chirped. "Just intercepted a message sent to Quartz. Transferring to your phone now."

I looked down at my phone. The message told Quartz to meet somewhere else. A sure way to lose anybody tailing him. Either they're worried—or they know we're onto them, which would mean someone is watching us.

Citrine watched him like a mama hawk guarding her chick. Quartz stood up and returned his mug to the owner. He turned his coat collar up and went outside into the night air.

"He's on the move again. We'll hang here for a minute and see where he goes."

Not wanting to expose Crystal, I had to ask, "How can we track him after a minute? He could've gone in any direction."

Citrine looked at me like I'd just spoken Klingon. "You know the answer to that one."

"Refresh me."

"I activated the tracker. Usually, we turn it off after a mission. But since I saw his ass, I turned it on."

"Will he know if you turned it on?"

"Did you know when Pearl turned yours on when we accepted this assignment?"

"How do you even know how to turn it on?"

"You've got that power too. All you need to do is go to your team roster, click on their profile, and turn it on. It only works if they're assigned to your team."

While we waited, the café owner came over with a package. His German accent was thick but we still understood him. He gave us a basket full of pastries and other sweets. We eagerly accepted the basket and gave him thanks.

As I looked through the basket, Citrine alerted me. "He stopped at a store around the corner. Let's go."

We waved to the café owner and linked arms again once we were outside. We engaged in small talk until we arrived at our destination.

I hesitated as I looked at the storefront. It was one of those places you entered deliberately rather than just casually browsed.

Citrine must've felt the same way because she slowed her pace and peered into the shop window. I followed her and did the same. What I saw stopped my blood cold.

There was Marcel—the man who'd bought me at that party. The man who'd once traveled to New Orleans with me and Silverback.

Now, I understood what everyone meant by this getting deeper than any of us could've imagined.

I nudged Citrine. "Hey, let's get back. Don't want the pastries getting cold."

Citrine nodded. "Agreed. We need to regroup or tell Sid what we've discovered."

We walked back to the house shivering from the cold and the revelation.

***

The sun woke me up. I stretched and prepared for the day. As I admired my outfit, I wondered what was in store for today.

I went downstairs on a mission to find coffee. I found Kora and Moons sitting at the table talking.

"Good morning! Did you want some breakfast?" Kora put down her cup as Moons smiled. She looked heavenly with the light shining, as if she was wearing a halo.

"Coffee would be great," I said, taking a seat.

"Where's everyone else?" I gratefully took the coffee from Kora and began to sip.

"Still asleep," Moons rolled her eyes. "Everyone stayed up last night after you went to bed. They ate all the pastries. I really wanted some of those cake muffins with the chocolate glaze." She pouted. Damn, I'd never seen Moons pout.

"Amerikaner," Kora corrected, jotting something on her pad. Then, as if something bit her, Kora looked up. "By the way, Onyx, there's a message for you." She handed me an envelope with my government name on it.

I flipped it over as Kora tutted. "I've already checked. It's clear."

I thanked her and opened it. A card was inside. It read nothing more than an address and these words: **Come see me. And come alone.**

My heart skipped a beat. The smell was so familiar, it took me right back to the Pride Room. Marcel.

No way was I letting Citrine know where I was going. The last thing I wanted was to pull her into this mess when I had no idea how deep it went.

I gulped my coffee, grabbed my jacket and shoes, and headed to leave.

"Going for a walk. I'll be back." I shut the door before anyone could stop me.

I went to the team roster and turned off my tracker. No need for Citrine to know where I was. I followed the address.

"Crystal?" I asked as I walked.

"Yes, Commander?"

"Go dark until I say so."

"I highly advise against that—"

"That's an order. Not a request."

"Understood." Then I heard her shut down.

I arrived at the same store where Citrine and I had seen Quartz and Marcel. I turned the knob and stepped inside. An old man sat at the counter, his eyes peering at me. I was about to speak, but he simply pointed toward the back.

While I walked deeper into the store, second thoughts swirled in my mind. *What if something happens? I've got no backup. Damn, what do I get myself into?*

Suddenly, a voice deep and low slid behind me.

"So, you came to see me?" The door clicked shut and I heard the lock slide into place.

Calm with a hint of edge. It reminded me of Silverback—his voice was one of the first things that attracted me to him. The hairs on my neck stood up as I felt the brush of velvet lips against my skin. Heat rose inside me as his hands wrapped around my waist. I felt so drawn to this man. His lips found their way to my ear. I had no idea what he said, but the sheer magnetism of his voice pulled me in. His hands traveled from my waist to my throat, slowly grabbing my neck, causing my head to fall back.

"Let me see those eyes," he commanded. Without hesitation, I opened them—and saw Marcel.

My mind screamed to institute defensive maneuvers, but my body wanted him to keep going.

"Ah. There she is. Not a thing has changed about you." He licked the tip of my nose. The flicker from his hazel eyes, the scent from his cologne, his voice with that accent—it was an intoxicating combination.

While still holding my neck, he bit my lip as I bit his. He kept me pinned against him, rendering me helpless. And at that point, I didn't care.

I slid my tongue into his mouth as he sucked it. He tasted like tobacco and whiskey. His grip around my neck tightened—enough for me to breathe, but tight enough to remind me who held the power. To anyone else, it might have looked like desperate passion. But beneath it was something else—strategy.

He whirled me around and pulled my hair so I still faced him. His eyes smoldered like a predator studying its prey. He bit my chin. "Not yet. I've got business to settle with you." He released my hair and walked back to the table. He dropped into a chair and sighed, motioning for me to sit.

Cautiously, I sat. Marcel lifted his hands in the air. "I don't want to harm you…well, not in that way." His grin glimmered like a row of diamonds.

I finally found my voice. "How did you know where I was staying?"

He rolled his eyes, as if my question insulted his intelligence. "Onyx," he said slowly, "as y'all been watching us, we've been watching you. I lost y'all after London, but one of my guys picked up your scent."

I blinked, shocked he'd used my code name. He'd always called me Jemeka before this. Now, the stakes were even higher.

"Why me?" I demanded. "Why follow me?"

Marcel leaned forward, bracing his forearms on the table. "Word travels fast when a woman takes out an entire Enforcer cell. Nobody's ever done that. And when my sources told me it was you…I couldn't believe it. I remembered you as the girl so madly in love with a man who didn't deserve you. You weren't the only one."

I rolled my eyes and leaned back. "Yeah, I loved him. He believed in me. Told me things. But once he saw I was independent, he got his crew to beat and rape me while we were thousands of miles from home. Then he testified against me at their court martial. They were found not guilty."

Marcel's face changed. For the first time, uncertainty flickered in his eyes. "I had no idea. I really didn't." He lifted his head, his voice grave. "Look at me."

I slowly raised my gaze to meet his.

"Tell me the truth," he said, voice low. "Do you still love him?"

I hesitated, then answered honestly. "Part of me will always love him. But in love? No." And that was the truth.

Marcel shifted, his stance softening. "I've always admired you. Even when you were with my homeboy. You just ooze strength. And I'm not gonna lie, you're sexy as hell. Which is why I'm coming to you."

Still unsure, I crossed my arms. "I'm listening."

Marcel sighed. "My crew's safety. I'm not selling out my people if it'll get them eliminated."

I shifted. "I can't assure anything. But depending on the information, I might be able to help. Why didn't you tell me this information in the Pride Room?"

He looked away, then back at me, his eyes narrowing slightly. "There were ears everywhere. Why would I tell you that then? Plus, I didn't know where your loyalties lay."

I tilted my chin. "You're in this game as much as I am. We both know there's no loyalty without leverage."

Marcel smirked. "Always loved how your mind works."

I let silence stretch between us. "Talk."

Marcel leaned forward, lowering his voice. "The disappearances? Not random. Your missing Navy corpsman and Marine? They witnessed something they shouldn't have at one of Nemean's parties. The Marine tried to leave. The corpsman tried to protect him. That's why they vanished."

My pulse jumped. "So this does connect to someone higher."

"And to your higher-ups," Marcel said flatly. "There are names on both sides playing this game. And it's way bigger than either of us thought."

I clenched my fists. "Why tell me?"

"Because I'm tired of cleaning up everyone's shit. Eventually, they're going to come for me and my Custodians. I'd rather choose my allies."

"And Quartz?" I shot back.

Marcel hesitated. "He's my man. He's gathering intel. But I think your side is catching on."

I narrowed my eyes. "We'll see about that."

Marcel leaned back and crossed his arms. "Here's my proposition. Let me feed you intel. Quietly. Help me burn their operation from the inside. And I'll help you close your case."

I stared at him. "You'd betray your own people?"

Marcel gave a bitter laugh. "I'm loyal to my people, not to a monster who treats human lives like poker chips."

I weighed the proposition. "I'll think about it."

He rose and gently touched my chin. "You do that. And Onyx…" His voice dropped to a sensual whisper. "Don't pretend you didn't enjoy that kiss."

He turned and disappeared through a side door, leaving me alone with the smell of vetiver and the echo of a thousand questions.

CHAPTER 7

The Pivot

I left the clock repair shop and headed toward Hafenhaus, my mind still tangled around Marcel's words. By the time I reached our place, only twenty minutes had passed—but it felt like hours.

"Crystal?" I murmured.

"I'm here, Commander. I compiled the notes from your meeting—excluding your higher pulse rate."

I rolled my eyes but stopped walking. "Wait. I told you to go dark."

"Go dark means don't speak but continue observing. Which is exactly what I did."

Relief washed over me. "Okay. So…tell me what you think."

"Tell Citrine what happened. She'll find out eventually."

"I know that part. I mean—what do *you* think?"

"I detected no lies from him. Though I'm surprised you managed to keep your pants on, considering he was definitely trying to hit it."

"Crystal!" I hissed, heat flooding my cheeks. "That's vulgar. And for the record, I'm a lady. I can control myself." I smirked as I kept walking.

When I pushed open the door to Hafenhaus, Citrine and Aster were standing there, arms crossed, scowling hard enough to crack marble.

Citrine jabbed a finger at me, then stabbed it toward the stairs. "You. Upstairs. Now."

I climbed the stairs like I was marching to the gallows. As soon as I shut the door behind me, the verbal barrage exploded.

"Where the fuck were you?"

"Do you know how long you were gone?"

"You better have been fucking somebody if you went off alone! Do you know how dangerous it is out there?"

The questions flew so fast I could barely tell who was saying what. I held up my hands. "One at a time!"

I took a deep breath. "I got a card summoning me to the old clock and watch repair shop we went to last night." I shot a look at Citrine. "Then I lost track of time because of what I learned there." I glanced at Aster. "And no, I didn't fuck anybody…although I was real close." I held my thumb and forefinger barely apart to show just how close.

Their faces relaxed a bit, and we all sat on our respective beds.

"Look, I get why you went dark," Citrine said, her voice dripping with concern. "But you could've told me."

"Please. You'd have been right there next to me!" I shot back.

Citrine shrugged while Aster burst out laughing. "You're right. Can't argue with that." She pulled her curly hair into a bun on top of her head. "So…was it Marcel? And if it was, did he smell as good as he looked?" Aster cocked her head, eyes glittering with curiosity.

I blinked at Aster. "You know who we're talking about?"

"Nope," Aster said, shaking her head. "But judging by your faces just from mentioning his name, that's all I need to know." Her eyes widened, eager for gossip.

I hesitated for a second. "Okay. Business first. Then explicit details."

"Business first," Citrine said sharply, sitting up straighter. Aster nodded in agreement.

I cleared my throat. "Marcel said the parties we've been investigating are tied to a trafficking network. That same general—the one from the Anger Corridor—is involved."

Aster's fingers stilled over her keyboard. "Holy shit."

Citrine's eyes darkened. "What's Marcel's angle in all this?"

"He says his crew is a cleanup crew. This general keeps screwing up and it's getting bad enough that it's messing with Marcel's people mentally."

"Wow. A villain with a conscience. Who would've thought?" Citrine quipped as Aster began typing again.

"That explains why witnesses and victims don't talk," Aster said. "They've been silenced. This dude is powerful."

"Even powerful men can be brought down," Citrine said. "There might be collateral damage, but if this prick doesn't live to see another day, it's worth it."

Aster raised her hand. "This mission is recon only. Before we do anything, we've got to tell Sid. She can give us next steps."

Citrine and I both scowled. Aster laughed and held up her hands. "I'm looking out for y'all! We have evidence, but we need something more concrete to tie everything together."

"Gives us a leg to stand on. Got it." Citrine rolled her eyes. Then she shot me a mischievous grin. "In the meantime…did he smell as good as he looked?"

My cheeks burned as my mind replayed the scene. "Let's just say…if we were in a different time, I wouldn't have stopped."

We all laughed but the tension snapped back as Aster's computer chimed. She blinked at the screen. "Oh. My sweep just finished." She clicked a few times, then her mouth dropped open.

"Y'all. Need. To. See. This."

Before we could say anything, she spun her laptop around. There he was—Quartz—talking with some of the higher-ups we'd discovered were part of the network earlier.

Citrine cursed. "Oh hell *no*! That twerp's been in our space, acting like he's one of us—and he's been with the enemy the entire time?"

I felt my stomach twist as I stared at the footage. *Damn it, Marcel…you left out how deep this went.*

Citrine spun toward me. "Wait…didn't Marcel say he knew Quartz?"

I hesitated. "Yeah. He said Quartz was…connected to him."

"Connected how, Onyx?" Citrine's tone went sharp as a blade.

I swallowed hard. "He…said Quartz was his guy. Feeding him information."

Aster's eyes went wide. "Holy shit. And you didn't say anything?"

"I was still trying to figure out how deep he was involved!" I shot back. "Marcel made it sound like Quartz was helping him track the network—not working directly with those assholes in the video."

Citrine threw her hands up. "So is Quartz playing Marcel? Or Marcel playing us? Or both?"

Without looking up, I muttered, "Why don't we ask Marcel ourselves?"

Aster gave me a wary look. "Can you even trust him at this point? If Marcel vouched for Quartz…how much does he *really* know?"

I stood up and stretched. "That's one of the questions we can ask." I headed for the door.

Citrine got up too. "Hold up. I'm coming with you. I need to make sure he ain't got you bewitched."

"While you two question him, I'll dig deeper and let Sid know what we've found so far," Aster said, fingers flying over the keyboard.

"Sounds like a plan," I replied, tapping my watch. "Time us." Aster gave me a tight smile as I shut the door.

Citrine and I were almost out the door when Peri and Moons intercepted us.

"Hey," Peri said, holding up a photo. "We got some additional info. Do you know this guy?"

It was Quartz.

Citrine kept her face smooth. "Yeah. He's one of ours. Why? What's up?"

I held my breath. We weren't ready to drag them into this just yet.

"He's been seen with another guy," Peri said, showing us another photo of a man with a gold tooth. I didn't recognize him but he reminded me of the country boys from back home.

"What's his angle?" I asked.

Moons chimed in. "There've been a couple of guys tied to him. According to people we've talked to, they've either paid witnesses off or threatened them to keep them quiet about the two missing service members." Moons laid more photos on the table.

My heart stuttered. One of the photos was Marcel.

Citrine and I shared a quick look, fighting to hide our shock.

I cleared my throat. "We've got to tell Sid about this. Get with Aster and help set up a meeting for tomorrow." I spun on my heel, Citrine close behind me.

A few blocks away from the house, the dreaded question popped up.

"So…how much did Marcel tell you about Quartz?" Citrine demanded, her voice sharp as cracked ice.

"He told me Quartz was his guy. That he had him embedded with us to feed us information about the network. I swear that's it."

"I'm not mad," Citrine said after a pause, her tone softening, though a flicker of New Orleans heat still lingered beneath it. "I figured you were hiding Quartz from Aster. I knew you'd tell me eventually. I trust you, partner."

We bumped fists and kept walking.

"So how we talkin' to Marcel?" Citrine asked, slipping into her city rhythm.

I kept walking and shot her a sideways glance. "I've got my ways."

We ducked into a small café and grabbed a table. I sent Marcel a message saying I wanted to meet. He replied almost instantly with nothing but coordinates.

See you soon, beautiful.

My stomach flipped, and I forced the reaction down. *Stay focused, Jemeka.*

I plugged in the coordinates. He was only two blocks away. I ordered a pastry and some tea. I wasn't about to jump just because Marcel snapped his fingers. We'd arrive when we were damn ready.

After we finished our snack, we hurried to the location—a flower shop.

Inside, an older woman behind the counter smiled and handed each of us a single rose. Without a word, she gestured toward the back.

Citrine and I exchanged a look. Hers was wary, all sharp angles and suspicion.

We stepped through a curtain into a small room fragrant with roses and lilies. Marcel was already there, lounging in a chair, looking as laid-back as a bayou afternoon.

Beside him sat a man I didn't recognize—tall, solidly built, the weight of authority rolling off him like summer heat. His gaze flicked briefly to Citrine, then back to Marcel.

A slow smile spread across Marcel's face as his eyes moved between us. I felt Citrine stiffen beside me, her arms folding tight across her chest.

"Ladies," Marcel drawled, his voice soaked in bayou warmth, smooth but edged with something dangerous. "Have a seat."

The other man rose and disappeared for a moment, returning with another identical chair. He placed it beside the first, waiting for Citrine to sit before sliding her chair forward with gentle precision. Then he resumed his spot beside Marcel, calm and watchful.

Marcel's eyes lingered on Citrine a fraction too long, and for an instant, something flickered across her face—resentment, or maybe old history—but she smoothed it away like it had never been there.

"So glad to see y'all," Marcel said, leaning forward, his accent as thick as Spanish moss. "What can we do for you?"

CHAPTER 8

Rose and Bone

"I wasn't aware you were bringing company," I quipped as Citrine sized up Marcel's guest.

"Neither were we," Marcel shot back with a grin, eyes flicking toward Citrine. He tipped his chin. "What it do, Cousin?"

"Not much over here but the weather." Her eyes never left the man seated beside him.

"Ladies," Marcel said, gesturing with casual authority, "this is Royce. He's my second. Anything you want to say to me, you can say to him."

Yeah, it tracks. I could smell the stench of womanizing, whiskey, and war stories thick between them. There was something about the way they leaned, the shorthand in their posture. I turned to Royce. "This is Antoinette. She's my equal."

Royce gave a slow nod and leaned back in his chair, thick forearms folded across his chest. Lord, I could feel the heat from over here. Citrine clocked it too—her shoulders straightened just a touch.

Marcel's hazel eyes gleamed like aged amber. He plucked my rose from the table and spun it between his fingers. *Don't look at his hands, girl. That's how you end up undone.*

"As much as I'd love to chit chat," he said, lips curling, "we're here for business, yeah?"

"Of course." I forced my gaze back to the table. "Let's get to it."

Royce slid an envelope across the table. Citrine snatched it up and opened it, revealing a dossier thick with printouts and surveillance shots. We skimmed it quickly—General Howard's personnel file, work history, and several damning photos.

"My crew's been dealing with General Howard for some time," Marcel began, his voice shifting lower. "He's got his hands in everything from trafficking to domestic violence, among other things. We're usually the ones who clean up the mess." His eyes dimmed, and for a second, I saw the wear behind the mask.

Citrine looked at me, then back to him. "You were the ones who silenced that Senior Airman? To protect his ass?" Her voice had heat. Royce didn't flinch.

"As if you've done everything by the book," he said coolly, his gaze like a blade. "Or agreed with all your orders. The ends justify the means, right?"

Citrine's lips parted, then shut like she'd bitten her own tongue.
Damn. I'd never seen her back down from anyone—until now.

"Look," I said, breaking the tension, "we've all done things we ain't proud of. No judgment. But if we're gonna shut this down clean, we need to know exactly what you were involved in."

Marcel leaned in, voice dropping an octave. "That's the case that bothered all of us. She joined the military to escape poverty. She only went to the party to meet people. Instead…" his voice trailed off. Their faraway stares and tight jaws said the rest.

Royce cleared his throat and picked up the thread. "Her story resonated because it mirrored ours. Most of us joined for the same reason—trying to outrun something. She was ready to testify, ready to take him down. And then… watching her light snuffed out like that? It went too far. Even for us."

As much as I didn't want to, I understood. Citrine shook her head, jaw clenched.

"So why us?" she asked. "If you're the cleanup crew, why not handle it yourselves?"

"You don't want it traced back to you," I added, watching Marcel carefully. "You're pulling strings in the dark, hoping we take the fall while you walk away clean."

Marcel stroked the rose petals with his thumb, never breaking eye contact. "Come now. Isn't this what you do? Go after predators, erase them without a trace? DS Enterprises has a reputation for finishing what others can't."

Citrine shot back, "And you have a reputation for making messes others have to clean up. We'd be stupid not to question your motives."

Royce's smile didn't quite reach his eyes. "You're right. We played a role in this. Which is exactly why we want to make it right by involving the best in the business."

Damn, he was slick. Marcel moved like satin. Royce, though, was tobacco smoke—rough, smoldering, and strangely intoxicating. No wonder they worked so well together.

Citrine snuck a glance at me. I scooted forward and locked eyes with both men. "You make a compelling argument. We'll consider it. But first—what about Quartz?"

Royce folded his arms. "He's with us."

"He may be with y'all," I said, leaning back, "but he betrayed us. That doesn't slide easy."

Marcel plucked a petal, tone even. "Then punish me, not him. He was under my orders. He should be spared."

My hand clutched Citrine's thigh, partly to ground myself and partly to keep her from leaping over the table. Marcel's "punish" triggered a completely different set of thoughts. Judging from the thigh grip she gave me back, we were thinking the same thing.

"Neither one of you walks away clean," Citrine said, eyes sharp as razors.

Marcel leaned over to whisper something to Royce, and they both broke into slow, wicked smiles.

"How about this," Marcel offered. "You finish the job. Then we talk payment."

Not taking the bait, I offered a compromise. "We're all Southerners here. Correct?" I shot a look straight at Royce.

Royce nodded his head. "From the mountains of Kentucky."

Ok. I'll accept Kentucky. "I know back home, my muh read the crab shells and fish bones. One thing she always said—*the spirits never lie when called upon.* Why don't we consult the bones?"

That silenced the room.

Royce shrugged. "I see no harm in it."

Citrine sucked her teeth. "Nothing wrong with getting confirmation. Who's reading?"

Marcel set the rose down and pulled a small burlap pouch from his pocket. "I got bones. Therefore, I read."

Citrine did a double take. "Boy, you carry bones?"

"Of course I do. Along with my gris-gris." He started to open the pouch, but I stopped him.

"Why should we trust you?" I asked. "Not everyone can read bones. And I don't need the spirits coming after me for a misread."

Marcel smiled. "As you said, the spirits never lie when called upon. Want to offer them a drink first?"

That eased my worry. Only someone *real* knows to do that.

"Any whiskey around? I'm not in the habit of carrying a flask." I tapped a rhythm on the table.

"Over in that cabinet." He nodded toward it.

I grabbed the bottle. We all blessed it and I poured some on the table.

"An offering given for wisdom received."

Citrine found some honey and drizzled it beside the whiskey. "To sweeten the path."

Royce reached over and sprinkled salt on the table. "For cleansing and protection."

Marcel added rose petals. Then he cast the bones.

The room fell into sacred silence.

Royce examined them, then looked to Marcel. Citrine's expression turned grave. I already knew.

"Quartz stays for now," Marcel murmured. "But the spirits agree—the General must be stopped."

"Indeed," I said. "And I just saw how. We'll contact you within two days. Do nothing until you hear from us."

Citrine tucked the envelope into her jacket. We walked out the same way we came in—focused, silent, and in control.

CHAPTER 9

The Last Visitation

The aroma of apples, raisins, and slow-roasted meat and potatoes greeted us as we stepped inside Hafenhaus. My stomach gurgled and Citrine's answered my call, making us giggle. We found everyone at the kitchen table: Kora and Harry fussed over the food while Reed, Aster, Peri, and Moons played a card game that seemed to be getting heated. Peri stopped arguing when she saw us.

"Hey! Look who's back! They'll help us decide!"

"Decide what?" I asked as I pulled up a chair.

Citrine grabbed a chair nearby and sat down. "Which TV show was better: Law and Order: SVU, Law and Order: Criminal Intent, or the original Law and Order?"

That one stumped me. I loved all three, making it hard to choose. But one stuck out to me the most. "Law and Order: Criminal Intent." I said decisively.

The looks around the room made me think I turned into an alien. "Are you nuts? The correct answer is SVU! The others are just fillers! Nobody says: ohh, I gotta go home to watch the latest episode of Criminal Intent!" The way Peri said that I couldn't help but bust out laughing.

Reed provided an argument. "Well, Peri, of course you would say SVU! You work in a SVU department. Onyx works in Major Crimes so it makes sense for her to like Criminal Intent. Personally, I like NCIS myself."

Citrine pointed to him with a wide smile. "Yes! Especially NCIS New Orleans and LA! But the best show of all time is CSI...with the original cast." We all threw our hands up in exasperation as shouts of *you got to be kidding me* and *hell naw* exploded in the room. From the corner of my eye, I could see Kora observing the scene with delight.

Harry, not to be outdone, stepped in. "Ok ok! All good arguments. But nothing is better than Matlock!" He spun on his heel with such a dramatic flair, I was surprised it didn't catch on fire.

Aster piped up. "I'm sure he watched Leave it to Beaver and the Andy Griffith Show as well." The room exploded with laughter as Harry's mouth dropped open.

"Ma'am! I am not that old! Although I do enjoy an episode of NYPD Blue every now and again." He put his hands on his hips and pouted.

Kora patted him on the shoulder. "Of course you're not Harry. But you are aged!" Oh my god! This house was on fire with the clapbacks. It almost made me forget about this afternoon.

Kora put up her hand. "Now, is everyone ready to eat?" In unison, we all agreed it was time to eat. Kora and Harry brought out the food with accompanying breads, cheeses, and drinks. Reed jumped up to help. I looked around the table and it looked like family. I caught Citrine looking at me with a nod. Yep, she felt the same way.

After dinner, the girls and I drifted outside for a smoke and a drink. The courtyard was quiet, lit only by a dim porch light and the fading blush of sunset. I figured this was a good time to update them.

I poured a splash of whiskey onto the ground. "For wisdom and guidance," I murmured.

"The contact we met with this afternoon," I began, glancing at Citrine, "confirmed what we suspected. General Howard's dirty. He's behind the disappearances and not just those two service members. There are more."

I sipped my whiskey and watched their reactions.

Moons took a measured sip of her tea, her eyes narrowing. "And you believe this contact? Can we trust them?"

"In this business, trust is a luxury," Citrine said, exhaling smoke from her cigarillo. "But the information lines up with Aster's data and everything you and Peri uncovered. It's consistent."

Moons wasn't satisfied. "Still. Why tell *you*? Why not handle it themselves?"

"Maybe they can't," Peri cut in, flicking her lighter uselessly. "Informants always operate at a risk. Sometimes the best they can do is hand it off to someone who can finish the job." Citrine leaned over and lit her cigarette with a soft click. Peri nodded, visibly calmer after her first drag. "Whatever you need, I'm in. Just give me the word."

Aster had been quiet, nursing her coffee, gaze far away. I tapped her thigh. "What's on your mind?"

She didn't blink. "Men like him shouldn't walk this earth. Especially not with stars on their chest." Her voice was cold, but steady. "They command those who protect our country. Abuse that power? They need to be put down like rabid dogs." She took another sip, crossing her legs. "Tell me what you need to make that happen."

I remembered the trauma she shared once—something dark that still clung to her in unspoken ways. And the fact that Aster wanted someone *put down like a dog*? Yeah. It meant she'd seen enough.

Just then, my phone buzzed. I glanced at the screen: an urgent message from Sid.

I nudged Citrine. "We've been summoned." I stood and turned to the rest of the group. "We'll be back."

"Hopefully with good news," Peri called after us. Moons just shook her head, exhaling smoke into the stars.

Citrine and I headed into the office, locking the door behind us. Sid's name flashed across the screen and I switched to secure mode. Her face appeared—sharp, composed, and unreadable.

"Is Citrine with you?" she asked.

Citrine slid beside me, now fully visible on screen.

"Good," Sid said. "Bottom line up front: you are cleared to eliminate. The best opportunity is during the Joint Services Yuletide Ball, which is in a couple of days. Connect with Opal for operational details. This needs to be neat. No mistakes.

Once it's done, you'll be extracted immediately. Is that understood?"

"Yes, ma'am. We understand." I spoke for both of us.

"Good luck, Commander." And just like that, the call ended.

The weight of the day returned, anchoring itself in my chest. Citrine placed a steadying hand on my shoulder.

"We got this," she said. "Ain't nothing we haven't done before. First light, we find Opal."

I nodded, and she slipped out to brief the others.

Alone, I sat in the stillness for a moment, then tapped into the comms. "Crystal?"

"I'm here, Commander. Something on your mind?"

"Yeah. This mission. I'm nervous... maybe even scared."

"That's a good sign," she replied smoothly. "If you weren't, I'd be nervous."

I let out a soft chuckle. "What am I going to do?"

"You'll lead. You'll execute. Like always. Only this time, it won't be with bullets—it'll be clean. Just like you handled Wolf."

That lit a spark. Wolf. Poisoned. Declared natural causes.

"Crystal, does General Howard have any health issues we could exploit?"

A beat of silence. Then: "He has a heart condition and Type 2 diabetes. If subtlety is your goal, an insulin overdose would be ideal. Virtually traceless. Easy to slip, no odor. Alternatively, a paralyzing agent could work—but it's detectable under scrutiny."

I went quiet, weighing it all.

"Commander," Crystal said gently. "No one can do this but you. You've proven that. Glacier and Sid trust you. Your team trusts you. So... why don't you trust yourself?"

I slurped the last of my drink and let her words sink in. They hit where they needed to.

"Thanks, Crystal," I murmured. "That helped."

"Always here, Commander. Let me know when you're ready to plan."

A soft knock. Citrine.

"All briefed. Opal's prepping the planning room for 0800."

"Thanks," I said, and sent a text to Sid. *Can I tell Citrine about Crystal?*

Seconds later: *Permission granted.*

I smiled.

Citrine stepped closer. "What's up?"

I pulled out the fob, popped in the earpiece. "Crystal, meet Citrine."

Citrine blinked. "The hell?"

"Hello, Citrine," Crystal chimed. "Nice to finally meet you."

She frowned. "Like Siri? Wait—when did you get her?"

"After my leave. Pearl had her built. She helped in the Corridor of Sins."

"Why tell me now?"

I gestured to sit. "I was ordered not to. But I just asked Sid, and she gave the green light."

She exhaled slowly. I continued. "You've had my back since Utrecht. You're not just my partner. You're my sister."

Citrine nodded, her face softening. "I couldn't handle someone whispering in my ear like that 24/7. But you? You can. You're the leader. Thanks for trusting me."

She hugged me hard. I held her tighter.

"Now, let's get some damn sleep. Big day tomorrow."

* * *

The next morning, gray clouds pressed low over the horizon. I padded downstairs, craving coffee.

The house was still.

I started the pot, savoring the rich aroma. But then—I felt it.

That shift in the air. A faint scent of damp earth. My skin chilled.

I turned.

Raven, leaning against the wall, arms crossed, a cruel smile painted across her ashen face.

I froze. I knew she was dead. I'd purged her from memory months ago. But she was back.

"What's the matter, Jemeka? Feeling out of your league?" Her voice dripped with venom as she strolled to the cutlery and picked up a knife.

My eyes narrowed.

"Guess Hell let you out today. Must be the stench of your rotting bones."

She tutted. "There she is. All bark. Never clever." She lunged—blade pressed to my throat.

"You're no leader. You're a scared little girl playing soldier. You'll never be this life."

Each word twisted deeper.

But I looked her dead in the eyes. "I may still hope for a prince. That doesn't make me weak. That makes me human. And I still believe in fairy tales."

I surged upward—raw strength in my limbs—and threw her off.

She hit the wall and shattered into a thousand pieces.

****

The alarm blared.

I shot upright in bed, gasping.

Citrine stirred. "You good?"

I glanced in the mirror. Sweat streaked my brow—but I was smiling.

A real smile.

"Never better," I said. "Let's go."

CHAPTER 10

Operation: Greenlight

The ball was two days away, both not nearly enough time to prepare and, for Citrine and me, too much time. Time only makes room for doubt. With rookies on board, I didn't feel comfortable tossing them into the ocean when they were used to creeks. I'd thought at first that they could handle it, but after seeing Peri's face, I had second thoughts. Her background was solid but we couldn't afford uncertainty.

Citrine and I agreed to scout the venue in person. Nothing beat boots-on-ground casing. Harry tagged along—his experience in hospitality would help us blend. He also suggested bringing Peri. Maybe walking her through the environment would ease her nerves. I saw no reason to say no. I'd rather babysit now than on game day.

Before we left, I told Crystal to go dark. She'd still listen and collect data in the background, but I didn't want anyone noticing her during recon.

We took public transit to the hotel. When the bus pulled up to the venue, we hopped off and stepped into elegance. Plush carpet. Grand staircase. Glittering chandeliers. The staff moved with polished precision, each one trained to serve without missing a beat.

Harry nudged me and whispered, "This is the crème de la crème of hospitality. The ball must be serious if they've got custom uniforms for the holidays." He nodded toward a group wheeling garment racks across the lobby—waitstaff uniforms decked out in Christmas motifs.

I whispered back, "Yeah, this party's elite. You can feel it."

Citrine popped in. "Why are y'all whispering? And without me?" She gave a teasing glare. "Yes, this ball is ultra-exclusive. Opal shared the guest list—top brass, military and civilian."

The glitz reminded me too much of La Puerta Obscura. It had all the same trappings of sophistication, designed to dazzle and distract. I wouldn't be surprised if something sinister happened during or after the event, especially after hearing Citrine confirm the names attending.

While I pieced those thoughts together, Harry and Citrine surveyed the exits. They weren't just marked—they were being *decorated.* Citrine pointed out that every door was trimmed with a bough of holly.

"Well spotted," I said under my breath. Citrine caught my eye, the corner of her mouth twitching in a silent grin as Harry led us toward the ballroom. Peri lingered behind, caught between awe and anxiety. I slowed and slipped my arm around her, falling in step beside her while Harry and Citrine forged ahead.

"What's going on, Peri?" I lowered my voice, keeping it just between us.

She hesitated, then exhaled. "Truth be told? I'm nervous. Y'all have done this before. I don't want to be the weakest link. Even Harry's done some high-level stuff. I just investigate. What am I doing here?"

Her breath quickened, shallow. I pulled her aside.

"Look at me," I said firmly. When she lifted her eyes, I guided her through deep breaths until her shoulders eased. "We all started somewhere, Peri. No one here came out the gate perfect. We *worked* to get here. You've got instincts. That's why you're doing coat check—out of harm's way. Reed will be with you. You're safe. I promise."

She nodded, then hugged me tight—tight enough to knock the air from my lungs. Tears pooled in her eyes. "You have no idea how much I needed to hear that. Especially from you."

I smiled and tapped her shoulder. "Even the strongest need a pep talk. Now dry your eyes. We've got work to do."

We caught up with Harry and Citrine without a word. Harry slipped right back into his rhythm. "Peri, here's the coat check. Your job? Take coats. Don't talk. Don't think. Just hang them up."

Peri gave a soft smile. "That's easy. I can do that."

"You'll be perfect," Citrine said, patting her shoulder.

Inside the ballroom, it was breathtaking. Tables glistened. The dance floor shimmered. Just like in the lobby, holly boughs marked every exit.

At the far end of the room, the head table had its own bar setup. I remembered from the seating chart: General Howard would be sitting there.

"Harry," I said, nodding toward it, "are the waitstaff and bartenders assigned by name?"

"Absolutely. I'll give you your assignments after this." He ran a hand over the table, his face suddenly distant.

I narrowed my eyes. "What's wrong?"

He blinked, shook his head. "Nothing bad. Just… remembering." He gave me a faint smile and squeezed my arm.

I rested my head on his shoulder. Citrine looped her arm through his, and her other around Peri's. For a moment, we were a family.

Harry finally spoke. "You'll be fine. One day we'll all sit around a table, good food and drinks in front of us, and laugh about this."

I kissed his cheek, then glanced at Citrine. "You already cased the bar, huh?"

She grinned. "Of course I did. All top-shelf. Crystal glasses. Citrus trays. The works."

Harry nodded. "If it's upscale, the bar is stocked with the guest of honor's favorites. We need to know specifics."

"Why?" Citrine asked, suspicious.

"So we know which drug works with which liquor," he said, lowering his voice. "Do we know the General's go-to?"

"Johnny Walker Blue. No ice," I said flatly.

"Perfect," Harry replied, grinning. "Strong enough to mask anything. Did you see any?"

Citrine's eyes flicked with memory. "Yes. It was there."

"Then that's our play," he said. "Waitstaff at the head table usually stay for two to three hours. After that, the formalities end, and the bigwigs leave."

"Which means," I added, "they're probably headed to another party. Like La Puerta Obscura."

"Exactly," Citrine muttered. "This place gives me La Dama Roja vibes. I thought it was just me."

"If that's the case," Harry said, checking his watch, "we've got less time than we thought. Staff orientation starts in three hours. We need to move."

We left the ballroom with just enough intel to confirm our suspicions and plot our move. No matter how elegant this place looked, something darker waited underneath the surface. The glamour was only a veil.

Once we stepped outside, the cold air slapped us. The sun shone, sure—but it was all for show, like everything else about this assignment.

We walked to the bus stop and waited. Harry cleared his throat, slipping easily back into his element. "Just so y'all know, security's tighter now that the event's so high profile. So, you've all got aliases." He handed us IDs as he rattled off the names. "Onyx, you're Cherise Simpson. Citrine, you're Dana Edmonds. And Peri, you're Cynthia Harvey. Keep your card on you at all times."

We nodded and tucked the IDs into our coats as the bus rolled up. Inside, we welcomed the warmth and quiet. The silence helped ease the weight of what we were about to do.

Mid-ride, a text from Opal popped up.

Change of plan. Briefing's been moved. Meet at the company's headquarters.

Coordinates followed. I entered them into my phone. Still on our route—four stops away.

Peri frowned. "That's strange. Why change it? And with little to no time?"

Harry leaned in, whispered something in her ear. She mouthed an "oh" and nodded. Citrine and I figured it was a security measure. Better to keep this off base than run everyone through clearance checks.

We got off and met Reed outside the building—he'd been pulled for security duty. A steady flow of people funneled toward a single entrance, so we followed the crowd.

Just before we reached the doors, Harry tugged on my jacket and whispered he was stepping around the corner to the café. I gave a discreet nod and kept walking.

The auditorium looked like an old theater; it had probably had a second life as a playhouse. We signed in under our fake names and slipped into seats at the back to be closer to the exits and able to see everyone.

People filed in like they were marching to something far more serious than a holiday party.

A pale, sweating lieutenant colonel took the stage. He looked like he'd rather be anywhere else.

He started with the General's expectations for the ball— then caught himself and swapped "Christmas" for "Yuletide." Then he muttered under his breath.

Citrine leaned toward me. "He just said this isn't his job and asked how he got stuck with this shit." She giggled, and I gave her a side-eye.

"When did you learn to read lips?"

"Took some classes back at the Complex during downtime. I know sign language too."

"That wasn't part of our training."

"Nope. Continuing ed. You should look into it when this is all over."

You really do learn something new every day. Still, as the Colonel droned on about protocols, my skin itched. Something was off.

He wrapped up and gave instructions for collecting name tags, uniforms, and assignments.

As I stood to go, my stomach dropped.

Quartz.

He was here—smiling, talking—with two unfamiliar men flanking him like old friends.

I nudged Citrine and gestured subtly. Her expression tightened.

She murmured, "Ask Crystal who the other two are. If they're tied to Quartz, then the gang's all here."

I nodded slowly. "But what's the play? Are they here to fix something? Or watching us?"

Truth was, some twisted part of me liked the idea of Marcel watching. The other part remembered—he answered to someone. *They* could be watching too.

Citrine raised an eyebrow. "Don't tell me you're thinking about Marcel."

"How'd you know?"

She smirked. "Girl, your face turned red and you looked far away. You always get that look when your mind's on something freaky."

"Focus," I muttered. "Let's get our stuff and head back to Hafenhaus. We can unpack this later."

"Should I tell Opal?"

"I'm torn. If we're being watched, do we really want her involved?"

"We can video her in. No need to have her show up in person."

We waited in line. Citrine messaged Opal. I scanned the lobby for more threats. Nothing jumped out at me.

I texted the crew: *Once you grab your gear, head back to Hafenhaus.*

Reed replied: *Peri and I will walk back together.*

Citrine linked arms with me as Harry texted one last note: *Be careful. Now's not the time for anything rash. In and out.*

We put away our phones and checked in with the waitstaff supervisor. Her voice hit my ears like a fork dragged across porcelain—shrill, clipped, and trying too hard. The way she barked orders made it obvious: she'd never been in charge before. Some people think authority means rudeness. In reality, it's just insecurity dressed in a name tag.

I caught Citrine's eye. She rolled her eyes and shook her head. Great minds think alike.

After her little "leadership" speech, we were instructed to form a single-file line to receive our uniforms, assignments, and further instructions. A buzz came through my watch—it was a message from Peri. She and Reed were done and walking back to Hafenhaus. Harry gave it a thumbs-up. Citrine pulled out her phone to text the group, but before she could hit send, we were hit with a screech that could summon birds from five counties.

"What did I just say? NO phones while in line!" The waitstaff supervisor stomped over like a deranged mall cop. Her voice screeched like a gaggle of seagulls fighting over a plastic bottle.

Citrine turned her head slowly, gave the woman an icy once-over, and calmly responded in French. Something about her child's babysitter and a fever. Her tone was sweet, dripping with honey but laced with red pepper flakes.

The supervisor's face turned pale. She backed off, mumbling something before scuttling away.

I kept my expression neutral, though I mentally applauded. *French? When did Citrine learn French?*

We made it through the line, picking up our uniforms, name tags, and assignments. When I was handed mine, the supervisor gave us a grin that made my stomach turn. The kind of grin that says *you've just been hand-picked for something slimy.*

"You two are part of the head table waitstaff," she said. "Dana, you'll be working the bar. And Cherise…" she double-checked the paper, "you'll be the General's personal server."

"Oh?" I tilted my head, playing with my ponytail. "Any reason I was chosen?"

She waved a hand and giggled. Her voice dipped into a whisper. "Oh, the General adores pretty things. When he saw your photos with the applications, he insisted on having you both close."

The faces of his victims flashed in my mind, each one like a ghost demanding justice. I swallowed hard, rage knotting in my gut.

"Well," I said with a smile, linking arms with Citrine, "let's hope we don't disappoint."

We thanked her sweetly and walked away from the table, keeping our pace calm until we hit the sunlight outside.

As soon as we cleared the doorway, our pace quickened. Citrine texted Harry: *We're done.*

Crystal buzzed in my ear, her voice sharp and deliberate. "Commander, message from Harry: Meet me at the café instead of returning to Hafenhaus. You're being followed."

I sighed and looked at Citrine. "Wanna grab something to eat?"

Her face relaxed instantly. "Girl, you ain't said nothing but a word." She held tighter to my arm, and we headed off, just two women strolling toward a café—like nothing was about to go down.

CHAPTER 11

Operation: ShadowGlass

For a Thursday afternoon, the streets were oddly calm – a little too calm. Part of me wished it were busier, making it easier to disappear into chaos if we had to. We took the long way to the café but I couldn't shake the feeling of being watched. Whoever was tailing us was patient. Methodical. Determined to keep us in sight.

The bell above the door jingled as we stepped inside. Warmth and the scent of roasted espresso beans wrapped around us. Harry was already seated near the window, half a pastry left on his plate, coffee in hand, smiling at something outside.

We slid into the booth across from him. He blinked back into focus and nudged a menu toward us.

"Go ahead and order. I know y'all are starving."

We both murmured agreement, scanning the menu. While I debated between two sandwiches, Citrine gave me a side glance and curved her lips into a knowing smirk. I could almost see the devilish horns sprouting from her curls.

"What's on your mind, Harry?" she asked sweetly, like baiting a fish. That was her move—curious and bold, always fishing for what others wouldn't say out loud.

Harry shook his head, lips still curved into a faint smile. "Some thoughts should stay private."

Citrine lifted her hands in surrender, smirking. "Fair. I was just wondering who put that smile on your face."

I laughed just as the server came by to take our order and drop off waters. Once she left, we circled back. With Harry, there's always more beneath the surface.

"Well, it's hard not to notice when you've got that beautiful grin," I teased. The sunlight caught his cheek, giving him an extra glow.

He blushed and patted my hand. "It's nothing. Really." He cleared his throat and shifted back into business. "Now, after doing some analysis…" He reached for his phone, scrolling through notes. "I got a ping from the tracker. Someone outside our network's been trailing you two. I sent it to Opal. She passed it to the Complex."

Harry's eyes flicked to me. "By the way, Jemeka, Amethyst told me to tell you that you could've invited her. But I told her straight—none of y'all expected things to go left. Otherwise, she and Lotus would've been the first boots on the ground."

Whew. I silently thanked him for covering me. Amethyst would've taken not being looped in personally. Truth be told, after working so many assignments together, I needed a break from everyone—even her.

Harry continued. "Anyway, Amethyst ran the signal. Here's who's been following you."

He flipped the phone to face us. My mouth dropped.

"That's Paul! I had a date with him—before Citrine and I ran that last case. He's here?!" I blinked, stunned. Then it clicked. Of course he was here. If Marcel, Royce, and Quartz were in town, Paul would be too. Marcel said Paul worked for him.

Harry nodded. "Been tracking you since London. Landed here about a week ago."

My stomach coiled. Citrine's face darkened with heat— New Orleans fire rising through her skin.

"So he wasn't in Brugge?" I asked, leaning in closer as the café buzzed around us.

Harry shook his head. "No record of him there."

Citrine snapped her fingers. "That's why Marcel said he lost track of you. But who knew we were going to London?" She paused. Her eyes narrowed. "Unless…" Her voice dropped as her jaw tightened. "Quartz told them. I sent that text to the team about our trip."

She cursed and slammed her fist on the table.

"Oh no, baby," Harry said, eyes wide. "Not this table. You know we can't afford German furniture."

That did it. Citrine sprayed water out of her nose. I cracked up at the sight.

"Stop it. I'm trying to stay mad!" she growled, wiping her face. Then she turned to me, all fire again. "Quartz is mine."

I rested a hand on her shoulder. "Let's do this first. Clean-up comes after."

Citrine rolled her eyes. "Fine. For your sake—and the mission's—I'll hold off."

I shrugged. "You gotta give him credit. At least now we know where his loyalties lie."

"To his detriment," she muttered, tearing into her pastry like it had offended her.

That was the thing about Citrine. Her passion, her conviction—it was exactly what made her so damn important to me.

I turned my focus back to Harry. "Are we the only ones being followed?"

Harry nodded. "Far as I can tell, yes. I'd bet they know about the rest of the team, though, but not what roles they're playing. And honestly—that's not a bad thing."

I glanced down at my watch. I needed to talk to Crystal. Harry didn't know about her, but as soon as I thought about that fact, I remembered Aster's upgrade—I could text her instead of talking out loud. A small comfort.

While Citrine and Harry playfully argued over which pastry was better, I typed a quick message.

Me: *Crystal. Do you have an image of Quartz and the two men who were with him?*

Crystal: *Yes, Commander.*
Two images appeared almost instantly, complete with data. *Reggie Brooks and Harrison Bell. Known as part of the Pack. Code names: Gator and Jack. Quartz is also part of this organization. Codename: Rabbit.*

I froze. *The Pack?* My pulse spiked.

Me: *Wait a minute. I thought I took care of them?*

Crystal: *You eliminated the Enforcer cell. The cleaner cell comprises—*

I didn't need to hear the rest. The images told me everything. Then the final photo appeared.
Marcel.
Royce.
Paul.
All listed with their codenames, neat as dog tags.

The Pack was bigger than I realized. How many cells were out there? My mind reeled. I needed to tell the team—but not here.

"Guys," I said, masking my tone with a casual smile, "let's settle the bill and get back. Kora needs help with dinner."

Citrine and Harry gave me puzzled looks but didn't argue. We paid up and left, stepping into the cold.

As the bus rumbled down the street, Harry glanced at his phone, then leaned in close, his voice low. "Follow my lead. Don't ask questions. Just do."

The sudden shift in his voice—the Navy command tone— snapped both Citrine and me to attention. We nodded, no questions asked. When you heard that tone, you didn't argue. You just moved.

Harry got off two stops before Hafenhaus. Just as I feared—we were being tracked. And Harry was about to lose them.

We caught our breath just around the corner from Hafenhaus.

Harry checked his phone and exhaled.

"They pulled back. For now."

We started to walk again but that nagging feeling scratched at my gut. I threw my arm up, stopping them midstep.

"Not yet," I said. "Let's detour."

I pivoted fast, heading the opposite direction. Harry didn't question it. Citrine gave me a look — the question already in her eyes, but she followed.

We ducked into a corner store. I pulled out my phone, checked Crystal. She flagged an unknown signal, too close for comfort.

How the hell were we going to make it back if someone was tailing us?

My adrenaline spiked — then leveled as a plan formed.

Citrine spoke low. "What's the move, Chief? We waiting it out?"

Harry's face was stone. He looked to me.

"You two stay here," I said. "I'm gonna see who's trailing us."

"Hold up." Citrine's curls bounced under her beanie as she shook her head. "You planning to engage?"

I placed a hand on her shoulder, steady. "No. Just recon."

Before either of them could object, I slipped out the door.

The signal lit up again.

And it was following me.

I ducked into a corner store and slipped into one of the aisles, eyes locked on the front door. Using the mirrors and window reflection, I scanned for whoever was tailing me.

There he was.

Paul.

So Marcel was watching me. But why?

As Paul moved toward my aisle, I seized him—spinning him, slamming him against the wall. He squirmed, tried to counter, but he wasn't trained like I was, not in this kind of hand-to-hand. When I tightened my hold, his resistance melted.

"Why are you following me?" I hissed.

He gasped for air. "It's not what you think, Jemeka—please, let me go!"

I applied more pressure.

"Start talking," I warned, "and I might."

He buckled, both physically and mentally. "Marcel's been keeping tabs since the party. After that night… after you and your friend met with him and Royce, he wanted to make sure you were safe. And to see if you'd follow through."

I loosened my grip just enough to let him breathe. "And instead of asking me directly, he sends you?"

Paul nodded. "Yes. If something happened, I was supposed to alert them."

His words hit me harder than I expected. Part of me was flattered Marcel still cared. But I pushed the thought aside and tightened my hold again.

"Do you know where we're staying?"

"No! I swear! I just know it's around here—nothing exact."

He sounded honest. Still, one more question.

"The two guys with Quartz—who are they?"

"Gator and Jack. We're all part of the same crew." He hesitated. "Are you gonna tell Marcel you caught me?"

I weighed my options. Killing him would set off alarms and tip the balance. He was a small fish. Better to toss him back.

"I won't say anything… if you don't."

I released him. He rubbed his throat, grimacing.

"Damn. You got a strong grip. I'll back off—but I'm still following you when you leave the house."

He turned and disappeared into the street.

I muttered under my breath, "How the hell are you tracking me?"

As I made my way back toward Harry and Citrine, Crystal came online in my ear.

"Your conversation with Paul, aka Coyote, has been uploaded."

I froze. "Pull records. Include Quartz in the query."

"Working on it."

"Thanks, Crystal. You're a real gem."

"A real one? You know fake ones?"

I groaned. Crystal played too much.

I entered the store and found my crew. "Coast's clear. Let's move," I said, jerking my head toward the door. Citrine and Harry followed without question.

We barely made it a block before the barrage hit.

"Girl, where were you?"

"What took so long?"

"Are you nuts?"

The overlapping questions made my head spin. I threw up a hand. "I appreciate the concern but let me be real—there's information I wouldn't have gotten otherwise."

Citrine did a double take. Harry steered us onto a quieter side street.

"Alright, spill it, girlfriend," he said, hands on hips, foot tapping like a drama teacher on opening night.

I burst out laughing. God, I needed that.

"You were right, Harry. We were being followed. And not by just anybody—Paul."

Citrine's expression shifted as the name registered.

"Paul," I continued, "is part of the cleaner crew. Codename: Coyote. So now we've got a Gator, a Jack, a Rabbit, and a Coyote. I'm guessing we're in the animal kingdom now." I tapped my lip, the possibilities teasing at me.

"Wait—Paul works for Marcel?" Citrine asked. "And Royce does too. Huh." She paused. "Why was he tailing you?"

I shrugged. "Orders. Marcel wanted to see if we'd follow through."

At this point, I didn't need to clarify what plan we meant.

Harry nodded slowly. "That tracks. Sounds like something we'd do with an informant."

Citrine wasn't sold. "Is that really all it was?" She raised a brow that could slice steel.

I started walking. "Far as I can tell. He seemed… low-level. More scout than hitter."

Harry buried his hands in his jacket. "Don't be so sure. Sometimes the quiet ones are the most lethal."

His words hung there longer than I liked.

Citrine broke the silence. "Can we go home now? I've been holding it in for an hour."

We cracked up.

"Yeah," I said. "Let's get you home before the street gets a golden shower."

Citrine smirked. "The street would be so lucky."

Peri met us at the door the moment we walked in. She grabbed all three of us into one giant hug.

"I was so worried! Glad to see y'all are alright!" Her voice cracked, and I swore I felt a damp cheek press against mine.

She gave Citrine and Harry quick kisses. Harry hugged her back, beaming.

"See? We're fine. Never better!" His tone was light but his eyes were already scanning the room. "Where's Reed?"

Peri smirked. "Reed and Aster are spending time together. Moons is napping. I just went through a couple cigarettes to keep from spiraling. Kora's out grocery shopping." She paused and glanced at the ceiling, like the names might drop down from above. "Nope. That's it."

I studied her face. "How are you really?"

She waved me off. "I'm good. Thinking back on what I went through to bring down a perp—this ain't nothing. And all I gotta do is wear a nice outfit and check coats? Please. Too easy."

I scanned her face for cracks in the smile. Nothing obvious. But something told me she was holding herself together with duct tape and bravado.

I hugged her as Kora walked in, arms full. Harry swooped over to help with the bags, earning a grateful kiss on the cheek.

Citrine turned toward us. "Do we need to go over the assignments? D-day is tomorrow."

I nodded. "After dinner. For now, we've got something else to discuss."

Peri raised her hands. "Say less. I don't need to be more nervous than I already am. I'll help Harry and Kora in the kitchen."

She threw us a wink, kicked up her heel, and sashayed out.

Once the door to the office clicked shut behind us, I locked it.

"Crystal," I said, "pull up the full roster. I want every code name from the cleaning crew."

A soft hum filled the room, then data blinked to life. Government names aligned with aliases. Marcel—Jaguar. Royce—Grizzley. Paul—Coyote. Quartz—Rabbit. Reggie—Gator. Harrison—Jack.

Jaguar, I thought. Yeah. Powerful. Stealthy. Sexy. It fit him.

Crystal kept feeding us more intel—roles, responsibilities, locations, frequencies.

Citrine extended her arm like she was trying to stop me from grabbing a live wire. "Do you see this? Look at the structure—it's us."

I peered more closely. The organizational chart stared back at me like a mirror. Cells instead of teams. Isolated, but united. No crossover, but clearly coordinated.

And that's when the memory struck. Glacier didn't want us touching this case. First at the party. Then after the briefing. Always recon, never engage.

"Why?" I muttered. "Why did our higher-ups tell us to stand down after we briefed them? Why is this operation so hands-off?"

Citrine cracked her neck. "Sid briefed only us. High-level eliminations? Those usually come from Glacier or Ruby." She rubbed her chin. "And no backup? That ain't normal."

I tapped the table, a cold sweat prickling the back of my neck.

"What if…" I looked up. "What if we're all part of the same network? DS. The Custodians. Hell—what if we're just different branches, all run by the same organization?"

Citrine blinked. Once. Twice. Then her eyes widened. "Holy shit."

My mind was racing. This information needed to be kept close to the chest. It wouldn't benefit anyone else.

I put a finger to my lips. "Not a word to anyone about this. Until we get something concrete, keep this between us."

"Agreed," said Citrine. "After we finish the task and get out of here, we'll have enough time to investigate this."

I turned to walk, but Citrine caught my arm. "Do we really want to know the truth? I mean… how deep does this rabbit hole go? I don't think it would benefit us at all."

"At this time, no. It doesn't benefit. But shouldn't we know what we're up against?" I searched her face for answers I wasn't sure I wanted.

Citrine sighed. "Let's do one task at a time. Our minds are already all over the place. No need to add more sauce to our chicken."

"You're right," I said. "Let's concentrate on the mission and getting everyone out safe and alive."

CHAPTER 12

A Quiet Psalm

After dinner and some light conversation, Moons suggested we give thanks to the ancestors—for bringing us this far, for the opportunity to forge new and stronger bonds.

Citrine and I had planned to do a simple ritual but truth be told, this felt better. More communal.

We gathered outside under the stars, each person bringing one ingredient to represent their mindset and their family lineage. The air was crisp, snow glittering like crushed diamonds.

Kora stepped forward first, holding bundles of sage and rosemary.

"To purify and protect the air that surrounds us," she said.

I followed with salt and cherries, placing them into the fire. "To honor the bitterness of this mission and the sweetness of victory. For protection."

Citrine poured whiskey into the flames. "To offer the ancestors drink as they guide us."

Harry held a honey dipper and let golden threads of honey melt into the fire. "To draw them near to hear us."

Reed stepped forward with juniper and an olive branch. "For peace. For clarity. For revelation."

Aster and Peri approached together, releasing six drops of lavender and peppermint oil. "For strength, for calm, for bravery."

Finally, Moons scattered lily of the valley petals into the fire. "To heal what must be healed."

We formed a circle, shoulders squared but hearts open, each person falling into their own rhythm of meditation and prayer. No words, no rush—just shared intention. Just silence, and the scent of burning offerings curling into the winter sky.

Kora stepped back from the fire and checked her watch. "Alright, people. Thirty minutes to change. We'll meet back down here for accountability. Don't worry about your things— they've been taken care of."

We quietly returned to our rooms. The tension in the house hung thick like molasses not yet cooled.

None of us needed the full thirty minutes. We were dressed and downstairs in no time, standing in a loose circle.

While Citrine reviewed the game plan one last time, I quietly slipped away.

In a quiet corner of the house, I was alone with my thoughts.

The possible dangers of the impending mission. Visions of Marcel's hands worshipping me. Silverback's velvet voice whispering, "That's my girl." Raven's cackle echoing from another world. The eyes of every team member, trusting me to lead them through hell.

I rolled my head back and took deep, cleansing breaths. My mind had to be clear for what lay ahead. There was only one way I knew how to do that.

Out of the corner of my eye, I spotted a small notepad and pen. I reached for them, settled into the quiet, and let my body go still.

As if in a trance, my hands scribed what my soul felt.

***

I'm scared. So scared
But I can't show it
Or let them see it
The sands squeeze through the glass
As the clock's hands tick our doom

Will we survive?
Or will we go down with guns blazing?
Our future isn't written on the wall
In fact, I can't see the future
We're walking into the viper pit blind

Maybe that's the best way
So there's no anticipation
We have our orders
Let's go

***

I stopped writing. I read the poem once, then again.
My soul felt lighter.
Cleansed.
Like a blade sharpened before the strike.

I folded the paper, walked it over to the fireplace, and tossed it into the flames.
The corner curled.
The ink darkened.
And the words were gone.

I gave thanks and slipped out of the corner to rejoin my team.

Go time.

CHAPTER 13

Operation: Holly's Fury

I rushed outside to see everyone loading into the van. Before climbing in, I wrapped Kora in a quick but fierce hug. She squeezed me tighter than usual—no words, just a knowing nod and a tip of her hat before she turned toward the DS building. Surveillance duty with Opal tonight. Her presence would be felt, even if unseen.

I yanked the van door shut behind me. "Am I the last one?" I asked, breath fogging slightly in the crisp air.

"As always!" Citrine called from the back.

The van erupted in short laughter, the kind people use when they need to hold on to normalcy. Then, silence returned.

The van was packed but quiet. Citrine sat cross-legged, adjusting her cuffs with slow precision. Aster chewed her bottom lip. Even Moons and Peri weren't cracking jokes. The only ones who had been on ops like this before were Harry, Citrine, and me. The weight of that wasn't lost on anyone.

To break the tension, I started humming *Carol of the Bells*. Citrine caught on immediately, then Harry. Then Aster. One by one, the whole van joined in, a low hum of breath and nerves syncing us together. For a moment, the fear fell away.

Soon, we reached the first drop-off point. Harry pulled to the curb and turned to look at Peri and Reed. "Be careful and good luck. We'll be watching."

Reed gave a nod. Peri flashed a thumbs up. I reached for her hand.

"Hey. You'll be fine. We got you."

She nodded, mouthing a soft *thank you* before stepping out. Reed hesitated a second longer than he should have. His glance over his shoulder lingered, unreadable. I chalked it up to nerves.

A few blocks later, Harry pulled over again. This was our stop.

Harry pulled the van up to the curb and placed it in park. For a moment, none of us moved. Citrine and I were seconds away from stepping out into the mission, but Harry's voice stopped us.

"Wait."

We both turned. He reached under the seat and pulled out a small black pouch. From it, he drew a pen—sleek, metallic, and cold as death.

He handed it to me without a word at first.

I stared at it. "This the one?"

Harry nodded. "Modified insulin compound. Fast-acting. Clean. It'll drop his sugar like a guillotine, especially after that whiskey you're giving him. By the time he hits the floor, it'll look like a textbook diabetic crash. No red flags unless they dig deep."

I turned the pen over in my gloved hands. It looked no different from the real thing. "And the real one?"

"Enlisted aide's got it in his bag. You'll see it tucked beside the snacks and water. Switch 'em when he's distracted. I tagged it with a red dot under the clip."

Citrine leaned forward. "How long once she doses him?"

"Seconds if he's already drinking. You'll have a ten-minute window max before someone tries to revive him. Just make sure no one has the right pen when that time comes."

I nodded slowly, the weight of the moment settling in. "Got it."

Harry looked at me for a long time, his voice quieter now. "Be careful in there, Jemeka."

I froze. He rarely used my name.

Then he gave a crooked smile and nodded toward Citrine. "Both of you."

Citrine bumped his fist. "See you on the other side, Chief."

I tucked the pen into my waistband, behind the fold of my apron. Then I pressed my forehead to his—our usual goodbye.

Harry did the same with Citrine. "You got this," he whispered. "Good luck, you two. Everything is waiting for you inside. We'll be watching."

We stepped out into the cold night and watched the van pull away.

I turned to Citrine. "You ready?"

She cocked her head, lips twitching into a grin. "Always."

Together, we walked toward the service entrance of the venue—two shadows moving into the firelight.

Chaos. That's the only word for it. The service entrance was a whirlwind of trays, yelling, last-minute changes, and too many bodies pretending they knew what they were doing.

I was this close to cussing someone out when Citrine tapped my arm and pointed. The supervisor. Thank God.

The woman spotted us and looked like she'd just been thrown a life raft. "Thank goodness you two are here! Dana, go with Stefan and the bar staff." She motioned toward a lanky man with sharp cheekbones and hair that probably required conditioner with a French name. His eyes were unnaturally blue — the kind of detail General Howard would appreciate. Beautiful and forgettable. A perfect mask.

"And Cherise," the supervisor snapped, dragging my attention back, "you're assigned as General Howard's personal server." She thrust a silver platter into my hands. "He wants everything served on this. He's very particular."

I didn't move.

"Oh my god, what's the problem?" she snapped.

I held up my hand, calm and sweet. "Do you have gloves? Since the general is *particular,* I'd hate to get fingerprints on his beloved platter."

Her eyes rolled hard enough to fall out. She rummaged through a plastic bag and slapped a pair of gloves into my hand, already waving me off. Perfect. Let the show begin.

I slipped on the gloves, took the tray, and headed out in search of the lead waiter. Halfway down the corridor, I spotted the restroom and ducked inside. Locking the door behind me, I whispered, "Crystal?"

"Now's not the time, Commander," she replied instantly. "There are eyes everywhere — even here. I'll advise you through your earpiece. Be careful."

I gave a silent nod and stepped back into the hall. The door had barely clicked shut when a hand slapped my ass.

I spun around.

General Howard stood before me, unsteady and flushed, reeking of whiskey. His eyes crawled over me like grease. He grabbed me with one arm, the other reaching to force a kiss. I slipped from his grip, giggling nervously, the mask sliding on just in time.

"Slippery," he slurred, licking his lips. "I like that."

He pressed me against the wall, his breath hot and sour in my ear. "Why you runnin'? I won't bite... unless you want me to." His hand gripped my waist possessively.

God. He really thought that line would work.

I let the fear rise just enough to make it look real. Widened my eyes. Bit my lip. "But sir... wouldn't it be better after the ball? That way we have all night."

His gaze darkened. He cupped my chin, nodded slowly. "Alright. I can wait." Then without warning, he shoved me harder against the wall and sank his teeth into my neck.

I flinched, a whimper slipping from my mouth. The pain bloomed instantly — sharp, searing. Bastard.

I knew this fear. The confusion. The sick shame. I had lived it before, and now I understood exactly what the others went through. But I couldn't freeze, not now.

"With so much going on, how will you find me again?" I asked, voice trembling.

He snorted, tapping the silver platter. "That's your homing device, Angel. Don't lose it."

Then he bit me again — hard — and stumbled away down the hallway, pawing the walls for balance.

I exhaled. My body still trembled but my mind had already reset. We had a job to do.

Crystal whispered in my ear. "Breathe, Commander. Use it. Anger sharpens the blade—but keep it steady."

I nodded once and pushed through the haze, making my way to the ballroom.

The space glittered with chandeliers that dangled like icicles from the high ceiling. Frosted boughs of holly draped the exits. Cranberries and silvery ivy curled around crystal candleholders at each table. Red fabric spilled across the floor and tables like blood in snow. It looked like I had stepped into a snow globe—beautiful, disorienting, and glass-sealed.

I spotted Citrine behind the bar, laughing with Stefan, her smile a little too wide, her posture too precise. She clocked me the moment I entered.

Her eyes sharpened like twin blades.

She stepped toward me as Stefan peeled off. "Who did that to you?" she whispered, voice low and lethal.

"Did what?" I asked, already knowing.

"Your neck," she growled. "Those *marks*—who the fuck—"

"Don't. Not now," I said softly.

But we both knew. Her gaze told me she wouldn't forget. And I knew this wouldn't go unanswered.

Stefan returned with a whiskey neat. "It's for her client," he said, voice slick with a practiced Spanish accent.

Citrine placed the glass onto the silver platter I held like it was radioactive.

I squared my shoulders and stepped into hell.

"Ah! There's my angel!" General Howard bellowed as he yanked me close. He snatched the drink and downed it in one go. His arm stayed draped around my waist like a prize he hadn't earned.

"How'd you all like my Christmas present?" he crowed to the table. God. What a pig.

Nine sets of eyes turned to feast on me. I felt carved open— filet mignon under glass.

"Maybe after you unwrap her, you'll be in the giving mood," one of the senior officers muttered, licking his teeth.

General Howard chuckled and looked me over again. "We'll see how the night goes." He turned back toward me. "That's all for now, Angel."

He slapped my ass and waved me off like I was some damn holiday centerpiece.

I turned slowly, each step calculated, the silver platter still in my hands.

That platter had to disappear. If it was his homing device, I'd make sure he lost the signal.

I walked back to the bar. Citrine looked relaxed, singing along to the holiday classics playing from the military band. As I approached, she caught my eye and mouthed "number four"—a signal he was on his fourth drink laced with the insulin compound.

I scanned the ballroom and spotted Gator, Jack, Coyote, Grizzley, Rabbit, and… Jaguar. Marcel. Dashing in his formal dress uniform, effortlessly commanding the room. My chest tightened. I needed to slip out before one of them saw me.

Shifting my focus, I tracked the general's enlisted aide. Sloppy and just as blitzed as his boss. I spotted the emergency kit tucked near the coats—exactly where I needed it to be.

At the coat check, I saw Peri. She looked alert, holding her own. Her coworkers, however, were already giggling and glassy-eyed.

I gave her a subtle nod and motioned toward the back. She followed me into the small storage room, where the General's coat and kit were hanging. I found the insulin pen inside, popped it open, and swiftly replaced the vial with the modified one Harry gave me. My fingers didn't tremble, but my heart raced.

We returned everything exactly how we found it and slipped out the side unnoticed.

Back near the coat station, I turned to Peri. "Is that all the guests?"

She nodded.

"Then disappear. Find Harry and get to your rendezvous point. Take Reed with you."

Another nod, then she was gone, weaving into the crowd like smoke.

I returned to the bar, waiting. Seconds ticked by like minutes. Then Crystal's voice crackled into my ear.

"Commander, Harry has picked up Peri and Reed. They're safe."

I let out a long, silent breath. One less burden.

Crystal's voice was calm but urgent. "Commander, dinner service begins now. Stay sharp."

The ballroom doors opened with a flourish. Uniformed servers flowed into the room like a tide, silver trays in hand.

The ballroom dimmed as the clinking of silverware and crystal glasses gave way to polite applause. General Howard rose from his seat, swaying slightly. The aide at his side steadied him with a hand to the elbow and whispered something in his ear. Howard chuckled and waved him off, raising his glass.

He tapped a spoon against it. "Ladies and gentlemen," he boomed, the microphone catching the edge of a slur. "Tonight, we toast to power. To legacy. To loyalty…" His eyes landed on me again. "And to the angels who make this life worth living."

Laughter bubbled up around the table as he downed the drink Citrine handed me earlier. I kept my distance, watching from the perimeter. The glass slammed down with a clang.

Then it happened.

Howard stumbled. His chest seized, lips parting in a confused gasp. The aide rushed forward, panic rising as the general collapsed against the table.

"Get the kit!" someone shouted. The aide fumbled toward the coats, knocking over a chair in his haste.

I slipped closer, heart pounding.

He returned with the emergency insulin pen — the one I switched with the concoction Harry gave me.

Howard's body convulsed once. The aide plunged the pen into his thigh, unaware of the fatal dose he just delivered. For a second, everything paused.

Then the General's body went still.

Gasps turned into screams. A woman in a sequined gown fainted. The ballroom erupted into chaos.

Crystal's voice slipped into my ear, calm and cutting: "Commander, exit now. Rendezvous in five."

I caught Citrine's eye across the room. She nodded. Showtime was over.

We made our way to the back, moving fast but controlled. As we passed through the kitchen, I spotted a sink full of steaming dishwater. Without breaking stride, I slipped the silver platter into it. It sank with a hiss and a clatter beneath the suds.

Took care of that problem.

We linked arms and walked quickly, the cold air biting at our lungs. Up the street, the black van waited like a lifeline. We jumped in, breathless, as the rest of the crew turned toward us with wide, alarmed eyes.

Harry didn't wait. He slammed the van into gear and peeled off.

"We're being followed," he barked.

Tires screeched behind us. A car was gaining fast.

While Harry was evading, I noticed Reed shifting and fidgeting uncontrollably. He cleared his throat. "Harry. They're after me. Let me out."

Harry glanced at him through the rearview mirror but said nothing.

"Damnit, Harry! Let me out!"

As Harry slammed the brakes and threw the van into park, Reed lunged for the door—but Aster grabbed him.

"Reed," she whispered, her eyes wide, her hand clenching his arm. Her face was full of confusion… and a silent plea.

Reed looked back over his shoulder and sighed. He smiled at Aster and then at Harry. Harry narrowed his eyes like a cat prowling its prey. "I'm so sorry." Reed stroked her cheek as if he was saying goodbye. He slammed the door and took off into the night.

Aster screamed as Harry turned crimson red and peeled off. I sat there in shock. What the fuck just happened?

Citrine said out loud what the rest of us were thinking. "What in the actual fuck?"

Harry said nothing. Moons was trying to console Aster, who by now was crying buckets. Peri just stared out of the window until she found her voice. "He said just run. Keep running. I kept looking back towards him. I don't know what I expected to see, but I didn't expect him to leave me like that."

Harry remained silent. Harry never stayed silent so long. I was worried. I inched closer to him and whispered, "what's going on?"

Harry leaned back, his eyes still on the road. "He was a plant. From them. I knew something was off when he arrived and no words from the main office. And we never do internships."

I slid to the front passenger seat, not caring if I was seen. "How long did you know?"

He waved me off. "I was suspicious in London but confirmed a couple of days ago. He would always wonder off, use Aster to get out of the house. I took my concerns to Opal, who then told Ruby." My head spun. Was Harry part of some secret mission? "My assignment was to keep an eye on him. Later, I found out he was part of the sleeper cell. If we didn't execute the General, he was going to do it."

"And they would've blamed us. We would've been hunted down."

"Precisely." Harry braked. We've arrived at the extraction point. Another van was waiting. I turned around and addressed the crew. "Ok, there's our van. Go quickly and quietly. The sooner we're on, the faster we can go. Understood?" Four heads nodded in unison. Harry nodded at me, and I opened the van door. They jumped out, Citrine going last. I shot a glance at Harry. Harry opened his mouth when, without notice, his head took a bullet.

"No!" I screamed, wanting help him.

Citrine came back and pulled me. "We've got to go. We've been ambushed!" She grabbed her weapon and fired back. My mind switched back to ops mode. I took Harry's weapon and fired in the direction while Citrine and I made our way to the black van.

We were ushered in by some operatives. "We got them all! Let's go!" The leader screamed as the wheels peeled. As we careened through the streets, I touched my forehead, feeling blood. Sorrow filled my heart again.

First, Emerald.

Then, Raven.

Now, Harry.

How many more lives would be taken?

CHAPTER 14

Operation: Fallen Star

I never thought an airport could be silent, but I guess there was always a first. Wordlessly, we remained silent as we hustled onto the private jet and it took off. Once safely in the air, everyone's emotions erupted.

Peri, Moons, and Aster cried silently. Citrine tried to hold it together but slammed her fist onto the tray table hard enough to rattle the drinks. I just stared out the window, watching the clouds blur past us like ghosts of what we just left behind.

A firm tap on my shoulder jolted me. A masked operative motioned for me to follow. Without hesitation, I grabbed Citrine. She grunted but followed anyway.

We were ushered into the back of the plane, the door shutting behind us. Two masked figures sat at a table across from us, then slowly removed their masks.

Glacier. Sid.

My breath hitched. Citrine exhaled beside me. Their pupils burned with fatigue. The whites of their eyes were red-veined, sharp. Alert.

Sid spoke first. "Ladies, I want to start by saying thank you. I know this mission was sudden, heavy, and abnormal. You didn't have your original team yet you still delivered. We appreciate you."

I nodded stiffly. "And the rest of the team? Don't they deserve your thanks too? They were asked to work outside their norms and did so without complaint. They need to hear that. Especially after—" My voice cracked. "Especially after what happened to Harry."

Sid nodded slowly but it was Glacier who leaned forward, her voice cool but edged with steel. "This was not ideal. And I know the loss of your teammate was deeply personal. You're not wrong for being angry. But I assure you, his death wasn't in vain."

Sid added, "We traced the breach. Reed was activated. He was a sleeper. Harry's death was the result of a takedown gone wrong. Someone from Reed's group pulled the trigger."

I felt the air suck from the cabin.

Glacier and Sid stood and left the room, leaving me and Citrine alone in the aftershock of their news. Citrine pounded her fist against the table again, knuckles bruised. Her jaw clenched so tightly I feared she'd grind her teeth to dust.

I grabbed her by the shoulders. "Do not fall apart. Not now. They're watching us."

"Then let them see." Her voice cracked like thunder. "Not all of us are like you. Some of us need to feel it or we'll explode."

I held her gaze. "You blame me. You blame yourself. Maybe even Harry. I'm giving you time. Grieve however you need to.

But when you leave this room, I need you composed. Like the captain I know you are."

She said nothing. Just nodded.

I stepped out and closed the door.

Then came the scream.

It shattered through the wall. Raw. Wounded. A cry you couldn't heal with time or comfort. I closed my eyes, leaning against the cold wall. I should leave her be. I should be strong.

But Glacier's words echoed back. A great leader always knows what her troops need at the right time.

To hell with appearances.

I opened the door and walked in. No words. I wrapped my arms around Citrine and pulled her into a bone-crushing hug. She collapsed into me, shaking. Together we cried. Each tear a memory of Harry. Each sob a release from the pressure we'd buried for too long.

Citrine pulled back slightly, red-eyed and trembling. "A remembrance for Harry?"

I nodded. "We'll do it. For him."

The silence continued as we journeyed to our final destination. I was relieved to see Peri, Aster, and Moons finally asleep. Even Citrine had her eyes shut, though her fingers occasionally twitched in her lap like she was still bracing for another hit.

I scribbled quietly in my notebook, trying to untangle my thoughts, until I felt a soft tap on my shoulder. Another masked operative motioned for me to follow—no words, just a silent nod. Drained, I obeyed.

When the door shut behind us, the operative removed her mask. I clapped my hand over my mouth.

Pearl.

We embraced instantly and the tears came all over again. Pearl held me like a mother would, whispering, "I know. It's okay. I know." Her voice cracked with restraint.

When we pulled apart, she gestured to a seat. I sank into it, still reeling.

"I didn't know you did extractions," I said, voice hoarse.

Pearl let out a low chuckle that somehow vibrated through my chest. "Of course. You're on my team. Why wouldn't I make sure you got out?"

Her warmth almost broke me, but my mind flipped into mission mode. "Sid and Glacier didn't give us the whole story. So… what happened? Why Harry?"

Pearl didn't flinch. She reached for a water bottle, offered it, but I waved it off. She took a sip and leaned back.

"We suspected Reed for a while. So did Harry. He kept tabs, and figured Reed wasn't an immediate threat. Meanwhile, I pulled Lotus and Amethyst. Got Garnet to assist. We did a quiet dig into Reed's background."

She paused to let that settle before continuing. "Turns out Reed is part of a sleeper cell in the Pack. They call it Viper Pit. His codename is Asp."

The name clicked instantly. My mind flashed to literature class. The asp that bit Cleopatra—hidden in a basket of figs. Beautiful, lethal, and patient.

"But why Harry?" I asked, even though my gut already knew.

Pearl's voice softened. "Because you were the target. The shooter didn't get a clean shot—so he shot Harry instead."

I closed my eyes. The fury, the guilt, the weight—it nearly choked me.

Before I could ask who, Pearl slid a photo across the table. A man with a shattered skull. Clean shot between the eyes.

"That's Mamba," she said. "Shooter. Pack affiliate. Garnet made sure he won't show up again. You owe her a drink when we get back."

My brows shot up. "Garnet's here too?"

Pearl nodded. "She was positioned as long-range cover. Just in case. Good thing, too."

She stood, smoothing out her jacket. I reached out before she left.

"Harry deserves a ceremony. Can you talk to Glacier?"

Pearl gave a soft smile, eyes damp. "Way ahead of you." And then she was gone.

***

Grey skies hung heavy over the Complex, casting a somber mood that matched the occasion. Even in Florida's warmth, the air felt thick with grief. We were an elite organization—

often scattered, constantly moving—but the pain of losing Harry brought us together. Everyone knew him. Everyone loved him.

We filed into the chapel in quiet procession, seated according to department. Pearl led Citrine, Amethyst, Lotus, and me to our row. Aster chose to sit with us instead of her section. Malachi came in behind, followed by Peri and Moons, who led their respective teams. The weight in the room was palpable.

The front row was reserved for the leadership—Glacier, Ruby, Sid, and Opal—who entered with composed solemnity. Kora and Io sat further back, expressions tight.

After opening prayers and soft hymns, Opal stepped to the podium.

"You know, there's a reason why Tennessee is called the Volunteer State," she began, voice firm but reverent. "It's a place full of people willing to give of themselves, to protect, to serve, to uplift others. That's who Harry was."

She paused, breathing through the tears building behind her eyes.

"The mockingbird, Tennessee's beloved state bird, is known for protecting its own. It sings for joy, yes, but also for warning. Harry was our mockingbird. Fierce. Loyal. Always watching. Always willing to act, even at the cost of himself."

Her voice cracked slightly. She looked upward, collected herself, and continued.

"Harry's legacy is not just in what he did, but in how he made us feel—safe, seen, protected. He was gentle, but firm. Quiet, but mighty. We will not let time erase his name."

She stepped forward, pulled a small flask from her pocket, and whispered, "Here's to a safe passage to the other side, friend. You shall be missed."

She placed the flask of honey wine in his casket, then gently rested her hand on the velvet lining before returning to her seat.

The bagpipes began their slow dirge. A single line of military honor guards stood at attention as Glacier took the podium.

She gave one small nod. Garnet stepped to the front.

Glacier's voice rang out: "Roll call!"

We all rose.

"Departments—report!"

Ruby answered first: "All sections present and accounted for."

Then Opal: "All sections accounted for."

Pearl leaned in and whispered to me, "You're reporting for Harry."

I nodded.

Sid's voice came next. Sharp. Commanding. "All sections, report!"

One by one, team leads sounded off.

Pearl stepped forward last.

"Onyx."

I answered. "Present."

Pearl called Citrine next. "Citrine."

"Present," she answered, her voice frayed but strong.

"Amethyst."

"Present," Amethyst's voice was full of quiet sorrow.

"Lotus."

"Present," barely above a whisper.

She continued through the rest of the names.

Then she paused.

"Harry."

Silence.

"Harry," she repeated.

Silence still.

I stepped forward. My chest tightened.

"Harry is not here," I said, voice thick. "But he's accounted for."

Citrine gripped my hand. Aster reached for hers. We stood together, unmoving, as a single tear fell down my cheek.

Sid turned. "All sections under my watch are present—with one exception. But he is accounted for."

Garnet turned to Glacier and nodded. "All sections and personnel are present. One not present…but accounted for."

Glacier gave a final nod.

After the roll call and final salute, no one moved. The silence in the chapel wasn't awkward or forced. It was reverent.

Pearl leaned over and whispered, "He's being flown to Winchester. Full military honors. The family's ready."

I nodded, my throat too tight to answer.

Outside, a black transport van waited beneath the swaying palms. A breeze rolled in from the Gulf, carrying hints of salt, citrus, and cut grass. Citrine, Moons, Peri, and Malachi stepped forward, solemn and steady, to carry Harry's casket down the steps. The flag over it rippled once in the wind, then settled.

Aster stood beside me, silent. Her hands trembled. Her face was stone. I watched her as closely as I watched the casket pass.

Once the van doors closed, the engine rumbled low. I stepped forward, laid my hand flat against the rear panel, and whispered:

"Rest easy, my old friend. Until the mockingbird returns to her nest."

The tires crunched over gravel and crushed shells as the van pulled away, disappearing down the winding drive toward the tarmac.

He was gone—but never forgotten.

CHAPTER 15

Burnt Offerings

With the weight of recent events, we were granted a few days of rest and recovery. I asked Pearl if Amethyst and Lotus could be extended the same courtesy, despite having been stationed at home base. She agreed and, for once, the entire team had the space to breathe.

But as the days crawled by, rest didn't feel restful. I felt caged. My apartment felt too small, too quiet, so I grabbed my keys and left.

The sun was shining, and a soft breeze kissed the city, but my spirit couldn't absorb any of it. I did the usual—worked out, burning calories and frustration. I wandered into Myrtle's Shoe Boutique and dropped far too much on boots I didn't need. Retail therapy didn't work either. Lunch alone felt more like punishment than a break.

When I finally returned home, Crystal chimed in.

"Hello, Commander. Glacier has requested a meeting with you at 1430."

I checked the time. 1355.

Seriously? Why couldn't anyone respect I needed time to mentally prepare for social interaction?

I groaned, threw on something passable, and headed out. After speeding through city traffic with the precision of someone who didn't want to get pulled over, I parked at the Complex and cleared security.

I made it to the command suite with six minutes to spare.

Jasmine, Glacier's assistant, glanced up from her screen and sent a quick message through chat. A beat later, she turned to me.

"She's waiting for you."

Her smile revealed the prettiest set of teeth I'd ever seen. Damn. She really should model toothpaste.

I stepped inside. Glacier was behind her desk, glasses perched atop her head, fingers dancing across her keyboard.

"Come on in. I'll be with you in a second."

Her tongue pressed into the corner of her mouth as she typed, eyes squinted in deep focus.

I sat and crossed my legs, scanning the familiar office. It hadn't changed—same pristine minimalism, same icy order. Except for one new item: a framed photo of a teenage boy with thick curls and features that resembled hers. A relative, maybe?

With a dramatic flourish, Glacier hit one final key.

"And that's that."

She powered down her laptop and turned her full attention to me.

"How are you really?"

Her voice was warm but measured—compassion wrapped in command. It always caught me off guard how she could hold both so effortlessly.

I shook my head.

"Not bad. But not good, either."

I took a breath, then another.

"Harry's death shook me hard. He was like a big brother. And now he's gone."

My hands trembled in my lap. I tried to will them still.

Glacier stood and poured me a drink without a word. She handed it to me and returned to her chair.

The first sip cracked something open. I didn't mean to cry—but I did. Silently. Grief spilled over for Harry, for Aster, for Citrine's fury and Peri's heartbreak. For the betrayal. For Raven. For everything we'd buried too deep and too fast.

But mostly—I cried for the truth: They were after me.

Through watery eyes, I noticed two things.

One: Glacier's worry lines were deeper today, though she still carried her youth like armor.

Two: She wasn't drinking. And Glacier always drank.

Something was off.

She slid a box of tissues toward me.

"You need to talk to Dr. Buho. In person, not just a quick telehealth check-in."

She raised a brow—half stern, half maternal. I nodded. She was right. Of course she was.

She leaned back, tone shifting.

"The reasons I asked to meet—I wanted to check in on you. But I also have some news."

That word always made me flinch. News. It never brought anything good.

"Before you give me the news…" I leaned forward. "Can we talk about the mission?"

She gave a subtle nod. Encouragement. Permission.

"What happened? Why was Harry the target? Why recon? And why did it take so long to eliminate this guy?"

Glacier sighed.

"Reed slipped through by claiming someone here had recommended him. At first, we thought it was Harry. But when we asked him…" She smiled briefly. "His exact words were 'hell naw.'"

I chuckled through the tightness in my throat.

"That's why Harry kept a close eye on him. We found out another group had infiltrated us again—this time through Security. Garnet took point. Dug deep. What she found…"

Glacier exhaled.

"There's a sleeper cell called the Viper Pit. Four members. Lethal. Bound by an oath—if one turns, the others eliminate them. The one who infiltrated us went by the codename 'Adder.'"

I paused. The name rang like a blade in my chest.

That's why Reed ran.

He had a change of heart.

And they killed Harry instead.

"So," I pressed, the puzzle pieces fitting too neatly, "if Garnet took out Mamba and Adder, only two are left?"

Glacier gave a slight nod.

"For now."

"May I ask what happened to Adder? Just… morbidly curious."

Without missing a beat, Glacier picked up a silver apple-shaped paperweight and tossed it into the air.

"He's been handled."

She caught it midair, her eyes never leaving mine. In that one gesture, she let me know it's none of my business.

Glacier carefully placed the apple down on the desk. "Was that all you wanted to know?" Glacier's face remained unreadable, carved in executive calm.

I exhaled slowly, accepting that was all I was going to get— for now.

She leaned forward, folding her hands on the desk. "Now for the second reason I called you here."

I straightened in my seat.

Glacier's voice dropped, steady but solemn. "Effective next quarter, I'm stepping back."

I blinked. "Stepping back from what?"

"From command. From DS."

The words hit harder than I expected. "Wait—what?"

"This wasn't an easy decision. But the time has come." She gestured toward the silver-framed photo on her desk. "That's my nephew. He's level two on the spectrum. His mom—my sister—passed two years ago. He's all I have left. And I'm all he has."

I followed her gaze to the picture. The boy's bright eyes and curly hair were striking.

"I've missed too many milestones already. He needs me present, not behind a desk pulling puppet strings. And truth be told… I need to remember who I am outside this building. Before it consumes me."

I looked at her, unsure whether to be proud or panic. "So who's taking over?"

Glacier offered a rare, soft smile. "Ruby."

Of course. Ruby. The only one with enough grit, grace, and fire to carry Glacier's mantle without dropping it.

"Does anyone else know?"

"Sid. And now you."

I felt overwhelmed by all of this. First, Harry gone. Now Glacier was stepping back. How would we still carry on?

Glacier's voice snapped me back to reality.

"You asked why we waited so long to take out Howard," Glacier said, her voice calm but carrying weight. "The truth is—we didn't. We were told to wait."

I narrowed my eyes. "Told by who?"

She paused. A flicker passed behind her gaze before she answered, her voice quieter now. "There are strings we don't cut… even when they're wrapped around our necks."

Something about this didn't make sense. I had to press. "You said we were told to wait," I repeated, the weight of her words finally clicking into place. "Told by who?" I asked again.

Glacier didn't respond right away. She reached into the bottom drawer of her desk and pulled out a slim, matte-black folder. No markings. No logo. Just clean edges and quiet menace.

She slid it across the desk toward me with two fingers, her eyes never leaving mine.

I stared at the folder, reluctant to touch it. "What is this?"

"Authorization," she said simply. "And a reminder."

I flipped the folder open.

One page. Heavy stock. Red ink. No name, just a jagged symbol stamped in the corner—a lion's jaw stretched wide, too wide, its teeth sharpened like blades.

I blinked. My body went still.

"Who… is this?" I asked.

Glacier leaned back, her expression unreadable. "We call him Nemean."

I glanced up sharply. "Never heard of him."

"You weren't supposed to," she replied. "Until now."

The silence stretched.

Long enough to hear the ice melt in my drink. Long enough for the hum of the HVAC to sound like a warning. Long enough for the folder between us to feel like it had a pulse.

Whatever this was… it changed everything.

I stood, folder in hand, the weight of new truths pressing on my chest.

Glacier didn't move from her seat. She sat there, elbows on the desk, fingers steepled, watching me with that unreadable expression that had once unnerved me but now felt strangely protective.

"Jemeka."

The use of my real name made me pause.

Glacier's voice was low, calm. Almost tender. "I know you're tired. I know this job asks for pieces of you it has no right to keep. But you showed up anyway."

A beat passed.

Then Glacier's gaze softened in that rare, almost imperceptible way. "You always did live up to your name." A small nod. "Tiger Lily."

I swallowed hard. The silence that followed stretched — not heavy, but full.

I didn't need to say thank you, salute, or linger. I nodded once, turned, and walked out with the folder tucked tight beneath my arm. Glacier's voice echoed in my bones like a benediction.

After my meeting with Glacier, I returned to my apartment, spent. I removed my earpiece and returned it to its fob. Just as I took a step forward, I nearly slipped. I looked down—an envelope. Plain, unmarked, but the unmistakable scent of moss and cedar curled up from it like a secret. A slow smile tugged at my lips.

Marcel.

I almost tore it open but forced myself to keep cool. Inside there were no words, just directions and a time: 2000 hours. I checked my watch—1700. Enough time to pull myself together. At least someone respected my time.

I texted Citrine to update her. A minute later: *"I'm coming over."*

She must've flown, because ten minutes later she knocked on my door and walked in like she owned the place. "Tell me everything."

I showed her the envelope. She studied the writing, then sighed wistfully. "I wonder if Royce will be there."

I snorted. "Still hot for Grizzley, huh?"

She shrugged, but her grin said it all. Before she could answer, her phone chimed. She glanced down, cheeks flushed. "I guess we're going to the same place." She held up her phone with a mischievous glint.

"At 2000?"

She nodded.

"Ride with me?"

"Thought you'd never ask. Can I get ready here?"

I raised an eyebrow. "Of course."

She hesitated, her expression shifting. "I never want to impose, Onyx. You've been through hell and back, and I know you need your space."

I placed a hand on her shoulder. "You're family. After everything—we ride together. You're not imposing. You belong here."

That broke the tension. I nudged her toward the door. "Go grab your stuff."

She cackled and swung the door open. Her bag was already there.

We ate, got dressed, and drove out. I parked a few blocks away, near Myrtle's. The address led us down a maze of alleys until we stopped in front of an old building with shuttered doors. No handle. Just like the invitation said, I knocked in the coded rhythm. The door opened.

A small elderly woman with thick white hair and a giant flower pinned to the side smiled at us. "Welcome to La Asfixia," she said warmly.

She introduced herself as Barbara and handed us each a flower for our hair. "This place was built in 1912. Back when folks like us weren't allowed in the fine clubs, this was our sanctuary. This and La Dama Roja."

The scent of rum, smoke, lemon, and fire danced in the air as she led us through. Ceiling fans hummed lazily. A pianist played something low and sweet. Bottles behind the bar sat label-less, proud in their anonymity.

She showed us the humidor—hand-rolled cigars, passed down from the old factory days. Pure tradition. No outside interference.

And then—our final stop. The private smoking room.

Inside, Royce sat with that knowing grin. Citrine's eyes found his and didn't let go. And there was Marcel. Rolled-up sleeves. Waves so perfect they could've been animated. Smoke curled from his lips. Everything about him said: I've been waiting.

Royce looked at his watch. "Right on time. Impressive."

"If the directions weren't so vague, we would've been early," Citrine fired back with a smirk.

I took the empty seat across from Marcel. He pointed to my hand. "You're empty. May I order for you?"

I tilted my head. "Depends. What would you choose?"

He exhaled slowly. "For you, cher, I'd order a Tempestuous Heart. A drink to honor the storm here." He tapped my chest—my heart, not my body.

I blinked. "Nothing tempestuous going on there."

He laughed, full and deep. "You know what I mean."

"What's in it?"

"Vanilla-spiced rum. Cream of coconut. Pineapple liqueur. Shaken and smooth."

I stuck out my tongue. "You lost me at rum."

"That's because you haven't had it right." His voice lowered. "I'd never give you something you wouldn't enjoy."

"And how do you know what I like?"

He beckoned me closer. I leaned in. He gently twisted a curl around his finger, letting it slide free. "If this small touch gets a reaction… imagine what else I can unlock." His lips brushed near my ear, not quite touching. I shivered.

Before I could respond, Citrine stood up. "This song," she whispered, pointing upward. "I have to dance."

Royce rose immediately and took her hand. Off they went. Gone.

Marcel's eyes didn't leave me. "Good thing you didn't ride with her. You won't see her again tonight."

I smiled. "I'm not worried."

He offered to order again. I countered—cigar for me, drinks on me.

"You know my taste?"

"Something elegant. Not overpowering. You like to stay in control."

He nodded slowly, impressed. "I do. So, what's my drink?"

"Rémy. Classic. Sophisticated. Balanced."

He clapped softly. "Perfect. But only if you try the Tempestuous Heart."

I sighed, knowing I'd lost. "Fine."

He ordered. When the cigarillos arrived, he selected one, clipped the tip, lit it himself, and handed it to me.

"Don't inhale. Just let it live on your tongue."

I did. The taste curled over my tongue like silk and smoke. Something in me softened. Opened.

"Now sip," he said, offering the drink.

I obeyed.

The drink and the smoke—combined—were magic.

Marcel pushed his empty glass aside, stood, and reached for me. I took his hand and let him lead me to the dance floor. The music swelled. His hands found my waist. Mine slid up to his neck.

"This is Cesária Évora," he whispered. "Sodade. A song about longing for home."

Something cracked in me.

I held him tighter. He kissed me again, deeper this time. It said we survived before asking what now?

I broke the moment. "Is this really just personal? No mission? No strings?"

His breath slowed. "You're looking for the lie. But this is the truth. I want Jemeka. Not Onyx. You want Marcel. Not Jaguar. That's who we are, right now. No masks. Just us."

"I don't want to get hurt."

He leaned in, forehead against mine. "Then don't run. Have me. I'm all yours."

My guard came crashing down. "Then take me," I whispered. "Show me who you are, Marcel."

He took my hand and pressed his lips into my palm—soft, lingering. Then he led me to the bar and murmured something to Barbara. She smiled and fished out a brass key from a carved wooden drawer.

"Second room on the right," she said, her thick accent adding to the spell I was already under.

We ascended the stairs slowly, methodical, not rushing. The air itself felt heavy with promise.

The door creaked open to reveal a king-sized bed dressed in rich cotton sheets and a regal blanket. The furniture was carved, old, but elegant. A bathroom sat off to the side, though I barely noticed.

From somewhere down the hall, I heard sensual, guttural sounds echo—Citrine and Royce, no doubt.

Marcel stepped in behind me, wrapping his arms around my waist. I turned to face him, and his hands roamed my body like he was tracing a map to a long-lost treasure. He stopped at my jaw, stroked my cheeks, and undid my hair. My curls tumbled around my shoulders, and the way his eyes lit up? Lord.

He undressed me. Slowly, thoroughly, reverently, until all I had left were my heels.

He scooped me up like I weighed nothing and laid me on the bed. I reached for his belt, but he stopped me with a firm hand and a crooked smile.

"No, cher. You first."

He slipped off my shoes, kissed the arch of each foot, then took my toes into his mouth—one by one. Watching me.

A moan escaped my lips, my head falling back.

"Let it go, cher," he whispered as his mouth and hands traveled up my body. "Stop holding back from me."

"Then let me feel all of you."

I sat up and unbuttoned his shirt, mouth seeking that spot at the curve of his neck. He tasted like warm spice and sin. I kissed, then bit. He groaned, low and hungry, one hand cradling my head as I pulled him closer.

When I undressed him, I did it slowly, savoring every part. The tension between us snapped.

What followed was heat and hurricane.

Breathless, desperate passion.

Gripping sheets.

Nails down his back.

Bite marks on my neck, shoulder, thighs.

Every thrust.

Every grind.

Every moan.

Like we were drowning—

And trying to save each other.

I think I saw heaven. Twice.

And when the storm calmed, we curled into each other. Marcel's head rested in the crook of my arm, his arms wrapped tightly around me. My fingers traced slow patterns through his hair, our legs tangled in a soft knot.

He murmured sleepily, "Now… that wasn't too bad, was it?"

I smiled, breath still shallow. "No. It wasn't."

"Please don't stop doing that," he mumbled as I kept stroking his head.

We drifted to sleep in each other's arms. No masks. No aliases. Just skin, breath, and the truth between us.

The next morning, I awoke to the smell of coffee and ham. I stretched, careful not to wake Marcel. It didn't work. His eyes fluttered open, and he did that newborn baby stretch that somehow made him look dangerous and boyish all at once. He blinked slowly, then smiled.

"Morning, cher. You sleep okay?"

The light catching his eyes was damn near erotic.

I rolled over to face him, tracing a finger along his collarbone. "I slept as well as you did." I kissed his forehead and he pulled me in tighter. "I do have one question, though."

"What's up?"

"What does cher mean?" I sorta knew, but I wanted to hear it from his lips.

He sighed as if used to being asked this question. "Oh, it could mean a number of things. Dear, love, cherished one. That type of thing."

"And how did you mean it?" I purred as I snuggled closer.

"My cherished one." He lifted my chin and gave me that slow, lingering morning kiss—one that almost led us back into the fire.

We were just about to go for round two when a sharp knock interrupted.

"Y'all up yet? I can hear voices!" Citrine. Nobody but Citrine.

Marcel groaned and shouted back, "If you could hear voices, why'd the fuck you ask if we were up?"

"Nigga, I was being polite! Anyway, breakfast is ready!"

I smothered my laughter in the pillow as Marcel threw a forearm over his face. "Lord, give me strength."

We untangled ourselves and freshened up—him in a crisp new shirt he somehow conjured, me stealing the shirt he wore the night before. When we stepped out, Citrine was already in the hallway, hair still a little wild but glowing like sunrise. Royce lounged nearby, a coffee cup in hand and no shirt in sight.

"How do you already have coffee?" I asked him.

He sipped, unbothered. "I move fast when I'm motivated."

We followed the scent of smoked ham and sweet preserves down to the small sitting room. Barbara had set the table with biscuits still steaming, scrambled eggs dotted with herbs, thick-cut ham glistening, and two little jars of honey and guava preserves catching the light.

The four of us sat around the table, the morning sun slanting through the shutters in streaks of gold. I watched

Citrine slather her biscuit with guava, Royce steal bites from her plate, and Marcel pour the café cubano with quiet care.

"So," Royce started, dragging butter across a steaming biscuit, "I heard the General croaked at that ball." He paused mid-spread, eyebrows raised. "Wonder how that happened?"

Citrine didn't miss a beat. "Whoever do you mean, sir?" Her New Orleans drawl rolled off her tongue like molasses, and whatever spell it cast made Royce grin as he tore off a piece of biscuit and fed it to her.

"He died of a heart attack," Royce continued, popping a grape in his mouth. "Complications from diabetes. Poor bastard. Who knew he even had it?"

I took a sip of the café cubano, rich and bitter. "Natural causes. Real shame." I forked a bite of eggs and let the sarcasm melt into the next breath. "These are good."

Marcel smiled, slow and wolfish, before kissing the back of my hand. "Barbara's one of the best." He reached for a slice of ham, but I caught his hand midair and offered it to him myself.

He leaned in, eyes locked on mine, and took the ham with his teeth—deliberate and sensual. "I love it when you wear my shirt, cher."

I smirked, wiping the corner of his mouth with a napkin. "And I love it when you smell like me." I leaned over and gave him a smoldering kiss on his lips.

After breakfast, we washed up and gathered our clothes. Marcel and Royce reappeared freshly dressed—new shirts, crisp collars, and smug expressions to match.

Citrine blinked. "Wait a minute. Where did those shirts come from?" Her gaze narrowed on Royce. "Last I checked, yours were in tatters from last night and I'm wearing your new one."

Royce chuckled as he wrapped his arms around her, pulling her close. "You lucky that shirt from last night wasn't my favorite shirt."

He kissed the tip of her nose and headed down the stairs.

Citrine called after him, "So which one's your favorite?"

Without turning around, he shouted back, "You're wearing it."

I looked over at her, and to my absolute delight—

She blushed. I think that was the first time I'd ever seen Citrine blush.

She definitely wasn't gonna live this down.

As he watched his friend disappear down the stairs, Marcel lingered. Then he turned to me, stepped close, and whispered in my ear, "Took everything in me not to rip that General's spine out when I saw how he treated you at that ball."

My breath caught. "You saw me?"

I thought I'd slipped away undetected. I saw him—but apparently, he saw everything.

Marcel's gaze darkened. "Wanted to see if he'd fall that night. It was perfect... like last night."

He closed the distance and sucked slow and deep on my bottom lip. My knees threatened to give out.

Then, just as quickly, he pulled back, his voice low and raw. "Until next time, cher. Keep the shirt."

And just like that, he was gone.

CHAPTER 16

The Lion's Shadow

After last month's rendezvous with Marcel, I had time to replay the meeting with Glacier in my head. The end of an era. If there was ever an end to the Ice Age, I guess Glacier picked the perfect time to thaw and walk away.

The folder on my coffee table haunted me. It looked like something cursed—Pandora's box wrapped in matte-black silence. Was I supposed to open this? What if I did?

I opened it anyway.

I spread the contents across the table. Images of a man with too many names and not enough wrinkles. Analyst reports with redacted passages and chilling timelines. And then—a partial client list. My eyes skimmed, then stopped.

HOWARD (do not touch)

I almost laughed. A quiet smirk pulled at my lips. Then it faded. Why couldn't he be touched?

My answer came fast and cold—he had access. Deep access. Intel logs. High-clearance files. Conversations that were never supposed to leave vaults. Howard wasn't the monster. He was just a pawn in a far nastier game.

"Crystal?"

Her chime played its usual perky tune—eager, waiting. "Yes, Commander?"

"What can you tell me about Nemean?"

A pause. Processing.

While she worked, I scanned the documents again. The further I read, the colder I felt. If you eliminated Howard, you didn't just unplug one man. You'd have to sever the whole damn network.

Fuck. This wasn't a cleanup. This was a war.

Crystal's voice returned. "As requested, Commander. You may want to sit. Considering the tension in your spine, I assume you're still standing."

I didn't even look away from the wall. "How bad is it?"

"Bad enough that sitting might help you breathe."

Her projection blinked to life, spilling across my blank wall like a commandment.

My breath caught.

Nodes. Threads. Cells. Dozens. Political. Military. Civilian. Each one had its own Enforcer unit, Fixer cell, Viper Pit, and something disturbingly similar to DS Enterprises.

All of it controlled by one man.

Nemean.

"Crystal," I said, my voice low. "Filter by active nodes. Military sector first."

"Understood." The projection shifted, lines collapsing, then expanding into color-coded branches. DS Enterprises flickered to the center, labeled *Field Node 19A*. Beneath it, subunits—*Cleaner Cell, Enforcer Cell, Viper Pit*—fanned out like a spider's legs.

"Zoom in."

Names started populating the branches. Some I recognized. Some I didn't.

"Do we have targets?" I asked.

"Affirmative," Crystal responded. "This list was compiled from Nemean's internal prioritization algorithm. Designation: *Tier 1 Kill List*. Would you like to view it now?"

I didn't answer. I just nodded once.

The screen blinked. A single line appeared at the top: **KILL LIST – LEVEL 1 CLEARANCE ONLY**

Then—

TARGET 01: MARCEL CHARDONNAY
(Codename: Jaguar)

Status: Active
Subunit: Cleaner Cell / The Custodians
Location: Unstable – under watch
Notes: *Insubordinate. Refused merger offer. Flagged for dissension.*

TARGET 02: ROYCE MCCOY
(Codename: Grizzley)

Status: Active
Subunit: Cleaner Cell / The Custodians
Notes: *Loyal to Target 01. High threat index due to influence among enlisted ranks.*

TARGET 03: HARRISON BELL (Codename: Jack)
TARGET 04: REGGIE BROOKS (Codename: Gator)
TARGET 05: PAUL WINTHROP (Codename: Coyote)

TARGET 06: OMAR JACKSON
(Codename: Quartz aka Rabbit)

Status: Embedded Asset
Notes: *Suspected double agent. Behavioral anomalies logged. Possible defection.*

"Pause list," I snapped.

My pulse spiked. These weren't just names.

They were *ours*.

"Crystal… they've marked the Custodians for death?"

"Correct," she replied. "Their resistance to absorption by Nemean's network was flagged as a destabilizing variable. I cross-referenced timestamps. The list was last updated four days ago."

Four days. That was before the ball. Before Harry was killed.

"What's the likelihood we're on the list?" I asked.

Crystal was quiet for longer than I liked. Then: "Higher than we would prefer."

"Show me."

The screen shifted again. This time, a new list loaded slower. Names appeared.

TARGET 07: ONYX
(Real Name: Jemeka Adams)

Status: Active
Alias trace confirmed
Notes: *Eliminated two cells. Refuses integration. Consider high priority.*

TARGET 08: CITRINE (Antoinette Benet)
TARGET 09: LOTUS (??? – info redacted)
TARGET 10: AMETHYST (??? – info redacted)

The names kept populating. The deeper I read, the more it sank in.

"Crystal, are we already being hunted?"

"Technically, yes. But informally. These are shadow orders. No official authorization. The kind that disappears if you succeed—or if you fail."

"What about Ruby?"

"Unknown. But she's not on the list. That… could mean anything."

I stared at the screen. At the blood-colored tags next to names I cared about. Names I bled beside.

"Print it," I said. "Hard copy. One only."

"Printing. Would you like it redacted?"

"No," I said coldly. "I want every damn name. I want to know who's hunting us. And who's next."

Curious about the military arm, I asked Crystal to filter for military sectors only.

The image shifted again—color-coded, clinical, brutal.

The Enforcer Cell appeared first. Government names listed clean across the screen: Silverback, Lynx, Wolf, Venom, Wolverine, Raccoon.

Status: **Deceased.**
Mental health status: unstable.
Cause of death: multiple. But each one was tagged… *"Linked to Operation Onyx/Raven."*

My stomach twisted. So this was what became of them. Not just killed—catalogued. Their deaths weren't accidental. They were *permitted*.

I moved on to the Fixer Cell. Jaguar. Grizzley. Jack. Gator. Coyote.

Then—Rabbit. Quartz.

I narrowed my eyes. The idea of betrayal from *that* kid sat wrong on my tongue. Too eager, too clumsy to be disloyal. But maybe that's what made him dangerous—he blended in because no one was looking.

I stepped closer to the wall. One name stopped me cold.

Cotton.

I didn't recognize it. The file gave just enough:
Status: DECEASED
Cause: *Internal conflict*
Notes: *Action authorized by peer.*

I tapped my chin. Internal conflict meant someone from his own cell handled it. Cleaner work that way—no need to outsource a correction. If one of them killed him, it meant he'd crossed a line the family couldn't protect.

I blinked slowly. Who pulled the trigger?

I pulled up the DS Enterprises arm next. My own damn house.

That's when it hit me—Glacier's words. *"There are strings we don't cut…"*

The approval chain. The vetting process. The ops we turned down and the ones we took. Nemean had the final say. Glacier wasn't just submitting reports—she was *asking permission.*

A pit formed in my gut. If we eliminated the Enforcer Cell, it meant they'd screwed up *so badly* Nemean approved their erasure. What the hell had they done to earn that kind of wipeout?

I started pacing. My bare feet against cold tile. This was too much. Even for me.

The world was cracked open, and the truth smelled like blood.

Sometimes, I thought, glancing back at the screen—

Ignorance isn't bliss. It's the only thing that keeps you breathing.

I stared at the wall a moment longer, the images still burning behind my eyes. Everything I knew was unraveling. But I wasn't afraid. I was *ready*.

"Crystal," I said, voice steady. "Send a message to Citrine and Pearl. Tell them a diamond has been discovered. They'll know what you mean."

"Message sent, Commander," she replied. "Citrine responded with a thumbs up. Pearl replied with the following: *Let's share the bounty in the vault.*"

I allowed myself the hint of a smile. "Copy all, Crystal."

I turned on my heel and rushed to get ready, grabbing everything that looked like evidence and danger.

Sid's office wasn't just the next stop—it was the war room now.

I slid behind the wheel of my jeep and peeled out of the lot, tires biting the asphalt.

Whatever waited at the Complex—I wasn't showing up empty-handed.

The moment I turned into the Complex parking lot, I saw her.

Citrine was just stepping out of her own car, coat flaring behind her like a cape. Our eyes met across the asphalt. No smile. No words. Just a nod.

We fell into step together, the click of our boots echoing in sync.

Jasper, Sid's ever-composed assistant, was already waiting by the elevator when we arrived.

"Ladies," he greeted with that polite smile that somehow managed to be both neutral and approving. "She's expecting you. Right this way."

As we walked down the long corridor, Jasper turned slightly. "Would you like any refreshments? Coffee, tea, something stronger?"

Citrine raised an eyebrow. "You offering rum in a command suite?"

Jasper's mouth twitched. "Only on Thursdays. Today, we have espresso and focus."

"Just water for me," I said.

"Same," Citrine added. "But chill it with that boss-lady energy."

Jasper chuckled, then knocked once on the frosted glass door. "Sid? Onyx and Citrine are here."

"Send them in," came Sid's voice, smooth as ever, but laced with something I hadn't heard in a while—interest.

The door opened.

Pearl was already seated, legs crossed, tablet in her lap. She looked up, face unreadable but alert. Sid stood behind her desk, hands folded, expression neutral. Her eyes told a different story. Sharp. Curious. Almost eager.

"Well," Pearl said, setting the tablet aside. "You've got our attention."

"And based on the message," Sid added, "I'm hoping this isn't just another coded flirtation with danger."

I walked in and dropped the slim manila folder on the table between them. "It's not. But danger might flirt back."

Citrine slid into the chair beside me, elbows on the table. "We found something in the network. Or rather... *someone.*"

"Ladies," Sid interjected. "Let's step into the vault."

She tapped a button on her watch. The bookcase to the left slid open, revealing a steel-lined door behind it.

Pearl stood and walked over. Sid keyed in a code, and the door clicked open. Pearl went first. Citrine and I followed. Sid came in last and closed the door behind her.

A whole secret room?

Damn.

It looked just like a war room—screens, a tactical table, thick silence. Impressive.

We found seats, and Sid dropped into hers with a practiced kind of ease.

"All right," she said. "Your move. What are we here for?"

Pearl leaned back, arms folded, eyes sharp.

My pulse spiked. Okay, here we go... but how much do I actually reveal?

"I'll be transparent," I said, hearing how hoarse and high my voice sounded. "If at any point I'm out of line, please let me know."

Sid leaned in. "Breathe. And you know we will."

I nodded and slid the file across the table. I included Crystal's compiled data—condensed, annotated, undeniable.

They opened the folder, flipping through the documents.

"Enlighten me," Sid said, still scanning. "What exactly am I looking at?"

I folded my hands, grounding myself in the chill of the table's surface. "What you're looking at is part of a network Crystal and I uncovered last night. It connects political, military, and private sectors. Each sector is mirrored—same architecture, same structure, different names."

Pearl's brow twitched. "Mirrored how?"

"Each node has four elements," I said. "An Enforcer cell, a Fixer cell, a Viper Pit, and something like DS Enterprises."

Sid looked up from the file. "You're saying we're just one arm of a larger machine."

"Exactly," I said. "And the one pulling the strings? Nemean."

That name changed the room.

Pearl leaned forward, the weight in her eyes sharp enough to cut glass. "I thought Nemean was a myth."

I ignored the comment and continued. "He's extremely organized. Each arm feeds intel into a centralized source. He authorizes operations. Glacier had to get approval for every mission. That's why we were always told it needed to go through 'channels.'"

Sid sat back slowly. "And the Enforcer cell?"

I swallowed. "Gone. Executed. Sanctioned by Nemean himself."

"Why?" Pearl asked.

"No reason listed. Just status: **Eliminated. Approved.**"

"And Glacier?"

"She didn't deny it. She just… passed the torch."

Sid went silent, flipping another page. The tension in her jaw told me she was chewing on more than intel.

Pearl lifted the next sheet and stilled. "Is this what I think it is?"

"The kill list," I confirmed. "Active. Prioritized. Includes military, political, and us."

I let that sit, spreading like wildfire through the oxygen in the room.

"Jaguar's on it. Grizzley. Jack. Gator. Coyote. Rabbit." I paused. "And us."

Sid's eyes rose slowly. "Define 'us.'"

"Me. Citrine. Amethyst. Lotus. Crystal flagged it last night. We're marked as liabilities. Designated for informal elimination."

Pearl set the file down gently. No reaction on her face but her fingers curled under the edge like she might flip the whole table.

"So we're expendable," Sid said, her voice cool. "And the people trying to kill us think we don't know it."

"Until now," Citrine added, her voice low and sure. "Now we do."

Sid and Pearl exchanged a long look. Gears were turning. That look meant war wasn't coming—it was *already here.*

Silence fell, but not the awkward kind. No, this was the kind that held its breath, that let truth settle like dust on polished glass.

Sid closed the file and folded her hands atop it. Her eyes drifted to the far wall as if she were watching a plan unravel in real time.

Pearl finally spoke, voice cool and clipped. "Do we have confirmation on how far this network reaches?"

"No," I said. "But based on the node structure, it's global."

"Then we're not just in it," Pearl muttered. "We're late to the war."

Sid stood, walked over to a cabinet, and poured herself a glass of water. No shaking hand. Just precision.

"This doesn't leave this room," she said. "Until I say otherwise."

I nodded. Citrine mirrored the movement. Her foot bumped against mine under the table—light, grounding.

Then... of course...

She leaned over, voice low enough to make sure only I heard:

"So... was this revelation before or after you were baptized by the Bayou Panther last month?"

I rolled my eyes. "Girl—if you don't—" But I cut myself off. Because the memory hit fast—his mouth, his hands, the heat still blooming in places I hadn't asked for.

Citrine caught the pause and grinned like she'd won something.

"Just saying," she whispered. "You seem lighter than air." Then she started humming *The Glow* from *The Last Dragon*, way too loud and way too proud.

I nudged her, trying not to laugh. "I came back with intel."

"And his shirt," she muttered.

Pearl cleared her throat. "Are we interrupting something— or do you care to share with the rest of us?"

Both her and Sid wore the exact same expression—stone still and unimpressed.

I waved it off. "No ma'am. Apologies."

Citrine looked down and bit her lip. Sid cut her eyes at us, just like Glacier used to whenever I cut up. Torch passed, alright.

"Ruby's my aunt," Citrine said, her voice steady but pointed. "She's capable of receiving information, whether it's good… or detrimental. Her approach may be more diplomatic, but she's just as calculating and direct as any of us."

Sid didn't react right away. She simply turned her head, studying Citrine like she was waiting for her to keep talking. "Explain."

Citrine drew a breath, not defensive—just certain. "This feels like a test. Like you think I'm trying to position myself against her by holding this information back. I'm not. I understand the seriousness of this network. But don't count my aunt out."

Sid's jaw flexed, something unreadable crossing her face. "You sound just like Ruby used to when she thought orders were optional." Citrine met her stare, unwavering. "Maybe she wasn't wrong."

The silence that followed wasn't just tension—it was memory, history, two women who'd seenthe same wars from different sides of the table.

The silence cracked like thin ice.

Sid leaned back slowly, arms folding across her chest. Her voice dropped a register—calm, low, but sharp as sleet.

"I know Ruby," she said. "We served together in Saudi. I also know she's your aunt. That wasn't a secret."

She let the weight of that settle before continuing. "But don't mistake leadership for ambition. And don't make the mistake of thinking I'm trying to take over." A pause, then: "Most commanders want the full what, when, why, and how. When we present this to Ruby, I want a couple of *courses of action* on the table. Options she can choose from. That's not usurping—that's *respect*."

She glanced at me, then at Pearl. "That is the mark of a good leader. And a better team player."

Pearl let the quiet stretch, then spoke—voice even but laced with something more grounded than strategy.

"We need cooler heads to face the inevitable. We're all on the same team."

I nodded, stepping in. "We need all hands on this thing. But the tighter we keep this, the less we feed the gossip machine. We contain the fallout by controlling the flow."

Citrine inhaled, steadying herself. "I wasn't trying to be disrespectful," she said. "My aunt raised me. After my mother was sent to prison… for killing my cousin. He was messing with me."

The room went still—not from shock, but from the gravity of that truth.

Sid gave a single, quiet nod. "I can tell the difference between disrespect and passion. You *should* have passion for family."

A long pause. Not awkward. Just necessary.

Then Sid cleared her throat and stood. "Stand by for orders."

Citrine and I rose in sync, giving them a silent nod before turning to go.

But just as we reached the door, Sid's voice stopped us.

"I'm damn proud of both of you," she said. "And it's an honor to have you on this team."

Pearl added without missing a beat, "You two are the best. The organization's in good hands."

I didn't look back. I didn't need to. The weight in those words carried all the way through the vault.

We stepped out of the vault and back into the hallway— same hallway, but nothing felt the same.

The air was cooler. The world quieter. Like the building itself had heard everything and was holding its breath.

I glanced at Citrine. She still carried that edge from inside, the kind that comes from holding your own against someone you once admired. Sid had that effect on people—she could cut you open and make you respect her for it. The balance had shifted, and we all knew it.

Citrine and I walked in silence for a few steps, our boots echoing off the marble.

Finally, she spoke, voice low but certain. "You think they'll actually follow through?"

I didn't hesitate. "We all will. Whether they want to or not."

She nodded once, just like I did earlier in the parking lot. Two soldiers. Same war.

Same flame burning in our chests.

No more secrets. No more waiting for permission.

The game had changed. We just stepped out of the shadows and into the fire.

And we weren't walking out of it alone.

www.ingramcontent.com/pod-product-compliance
Lightning Source LLC
Chambersburg PA
CBHW071454140726
47997CB00005B/1718